The Magic Ring of Brodgar

Book one: THE INHERITANCE

KATELYN EMILIA NOVAK

ARCHWAY PUBLISHING

Copyright © 2021 Katelyn Emilia Novak.

All rights reserved. No part of this book may be used or reproduced by any means, graphic, electronic, or mechanical, including photocopying, recording, taping or by any information storage retrieval system without the written permission of the author except in the case of brief quotations embodied in critical articles and reviews.

This is a work of fiction. All of the characters, names, incidents, organizations, and dialogue in this novel are either the products of the author's imagination or are used fictitiously.

Archway Publishing books may be ordered through booksellers or by contacting:

Archway Publishing
1663 Liberty Drive
Bloomington, IN 47403
www.archwaypublishing.com
844-669-3957

Because of the dynamic nature of the Internet, any web addresses or links contained in this book may have changed since publication and may no longer be valid. The views expressed in this work are solely those of the author and do not necessarily reflect the views of the publisher, and the publisher hereby disclaims any responsibility for them.

Any people depicted in stock imagery provided by Getty Images are models, and such images are being used for illustrative purposes only. Certain stock imagery © Getty Images.

ISBN: 978-1-6657-1350-4 (sc)
ISBN: 978-1-6657-1349-8 (hc)
ISBN: 978-1-6657-1351-1 (e)

Library of Congress Control Number: 2021920616

Print information available on the last page.

Archway Publishing rev. date: 07/01/2024

BOOK ONE
The Inheritance

PROLOGUE

June of 2016 proved to be unusually cold in Great Britain. The last suitcase was packed, and the path to Scotland lay ahead - Megan's ancestral home, yet a place she has never known. With a sense of longing, she looked out the window, where the rain had been falling incessantly for days on end. Her gaze then swept over her favorite room in the cozy Chelsea apartment, where she had spent most of her life with her mother, until she got married and moved to America, leaving her daughter behind. Megan was just nineteen when she found herself completely alone in London - a young woman in the heart of a vast metropolis. By the age of twenty-five, she had learned to live independently and handle all the challenges that life presented.

The day before, she received a call from Thurso, a town at the northernmost tip of Scotland, informing her that her grandfather, Malcolm, the patriarch of the McKenzie clan, had passed away. This clan had been deeply respected in the north since the medieval era.

Twenty - five years prior, following a bitter dispute with her father, Megan's pregnant mother, Arline, left her family home for good, moving to London and severing all ties with

Malcolm. Over the years, reconciliation remained elusive. Even on his deathbed, the elder McKenzie could not forgive his daughter, leaving Arline with nothing in his will but regrets over the family discord. However, he harbored a deep affection for his granddaughter Megan, with whom he kept regular contact, and to whom he bequeathed his entire fortune, including an ancient castle and a thriving whiskey distillery.

Megan was unaware of both the ancestral home and the distillery that had now come into her possession. She only knew that her grandfather's passing marked a profound loss for her. The next step was to venture to Thurso and decide what to do with the inheritance.

1
The Arrival

The trip proved to be quite challenging. After flying to Inverness, Megan boarded a train for an additional four-hour journey. She was pleasantly surprised by the stunning landscapes for which Scotland is renowned. The view from the window showcased mountains, crystal-clear lakes, scenic beaches, and ancient castles, each with its own secrets. Admiring the scenery, she became lost in thoughts about the future and didn't notice how quickly time flew by. There were very few people at the small station, but Megan immediately noticed a man in his sixties rushing to meet her — a silver-haired gentleman with a kind expression.

"Miss McKenzie?" he inquired.

"Mr. Douglas?" Megan responded.

"Welcome to Scotland! I hope your journey wasn't too exhausting, despite the distance?"

He greeted her with a warm, paternal smile and shook Megan's hand. She appeared quite youthful to him. The girl was of modest height, with a slender waist and lean legs. Her large, expressive brown eyes and thick chestnut locks of hair, both typical traits of the McKenzie clan, were certainly distinguishing. Her delicate build and facial features gave Megan a porcelain, doll-like appearance. She was dressed in a formal dark pantsuit that elegantly complemented her slim figure. Simple shoes with modest heels completed the young woman's business-like, sophisticated look — just as Malcolm had described his granddaughter.

"All is well, thank you," she took in the small railway station with a quick glance. Judging her surroundings, Megan quickly surmised that this was not a town but a village.

"I'm delighted by your arrival and our acquaintance. I've heard much about you from your grandfather," the silver-haired man said as he carefully placed Megan's suitcases in the trunk of the car. "He was very proud of you. I've spent a large part of my life by his side, always as his loyal friend and the family's solicitor."

"Thank you, Mr. Douglas. I'm glad to meet you too," she said politely.

"Allow me to escort you to the castle, Miss McKenzie."

"Please, just call me Megan."

"As you wish, Megan."

"Have we far to go?"

"About thirty minutes. Tomorrow morning at 10, your relatives will be waiting for you in the meeting hall."

"Is anyone currently living in my grandfather's house?"

"Yes, your cousin Warren and his wife are there, along with the estate manager. The couple had to leave for urgent matters right after the funeral, so they'll be returning late.

It's unlikely you'll meet them today, but there should be an opportunity tomorrow morning."
"I see. Thank you."

*****

"My goodness! It's gorgeous! I could never have imagined seeing such a delightful place," Megan exclaimed in awe as she stepped out of Mr. Douglas's car.

Before her, stood an extraordinarily beautiful castle. Its last renovation was completed in 1768. Over the centuries, the interior decor changed and improved with the latest technologies, while the exterior maintained its historical appearance, as depicted in pictures and postcards dedicated to medieval Scotland.

The castle was perched on a hill, offering breathtaking views of cliffs and mountains stretching into the North Sea. The magnificent green landscape extended for miles around. The estate was meticulously maintained, Megan noted immediately. Near the massive entrance door stood the manager, observing Megan intently.

"Good evening, Gregor!" she greeted, eyeing the tall, lean middle-aged man in a formal grey suit. He was exactly as her grandfather had described in his stories. Gregor's face seemed impassive and even stern, perhaps due to his thinness and lack of smile.

"Good evening, Miss. Welcome."

Malcolm had greatly valued the estate manager for his impeccable manners, respectfulness, discretion, and cool, calculated intellect. He was one of those individuals who spoke little but listened much. When the distillery faced a downturn, it was Gregor who secured lucrative contracts with partners. Now, he was in charge of communication with the main whiskey buyers, working in tandem with Megan's cousin Warren, whom Malcolm had recently involved in the business affairs.

Gregor took two suitcases from Mr. Douglas and led the way inside.

As Megan entered the mansion through the grand doors, she paused, taking in the interior with interest, which blended modernity with history. The original stone walls were adorned with numerous hunting trophies.

"Deer hunting has long been considered a noble pursuit for true gentlemen, such as your grandfather," Mr. Douglas explained, noticing Megan's surprised examination of the hall's unique decor.

"Are there bears around here?" Megan inquired warily, noticing a bear skin by the fireplace.

The manager smiled at her question, "No, that skin was a gift to your grandfather from an American hunter, an old friend of his."

"That's good…" replied Megan thoughtfully. She had always been afraid of wild animals.

"One need not fear the beasts," Gregor unexpectedly interjected, his gaze inscrutable as he looked at her. "Often, it is people who pose the greater threat…"

Megan scrutinized his face with a mixture of curiosity and suspicion. His last remark seemed odd, even menacing. Deciding she might be reading too much into his words, she chose to remain silent and turned her attention back to the hall's interior.

The chairs and sofa were upholstered in wool fabric made at the McKenzie mill, featuring the family's traditional blue-green tartan. Legend has it that this pattern and color scheme were adopted by the clan chief and his kin in the 13th century. Consequently, it had become a tradition for all family members to own several items in the blue-green tartan, for holidays, significant events, and everyday wear, suitable for any weather.

Megan's initial impressions of her ancestral castle were undeniably profound. A bittersweet melancholy washed over her as she realized that, despite the years which have passed by, she had never once made the effort to visit and see everything with her own eyes, to feel the deep connection to her lineage.

All these years, Arline had painted these places as a godforsaken backwater, untouched by civilization. Megan had imagined nothing more than crumbling walls of an ancient castle, frozen ruins on the verge of turning to dust, a vague memory of a glorious past. Now, she understood that her previous notions bore no resemblance to reality.

A grand staircase led upwards from the hall. She approached it, touching the cold stone balustrades. The center of it was carpeted with dense wool, also in the McKenzie tartan style, as was the furniture. Twenty steps led to the second floor, where the bedrooms were located.

"I wasn't sure which room you would prefer," Gregor said, "so we've prepared two options for you – your grandfather's chamber and your mother's former bedroom."

"I'll stay in my mother's room," Megan replied, thinking that she likely wouldn't be able to sleep peacefully in her grandfather's chamber. Despite being 25, she still harbored a fear of something unexplainable associated with the dark. Megan occasionally chuckled at herself for this; after all, she was an adult, a capable woman who could quickly find a way out of any difficult situation while maintaining complete composure. Yet, she was still afraid of the dark, ghosts, and horror movies, just like a little girl!

The castle is probably filled with the ghosts of ancestors, she thought, and immediately tried to dispel this notion to avoid scaring herself.

On the second floor, two corridors branched off from the staircase, one to the right and one to the left, with bedrooms lining both.

"The second door on the left," directed Gregor.

Arline's chamber, was both cozy and spacious. To the right from the entrance stood a king-sized bed made of mahogany, covered with a white down comforter and topped with a woolen blanket in the recognizable family colors.

Everything in one style, Megan thought, and she found it very appealing.

In front of the bed was a wide, large fireplace, above which hung a set of bagpipes — the national musical instrument of Scotland — mounted on the wall. The room, situated in a corner of the mansion, was one of the brightest in the castle thanks to two tall windows. Between them, there was a small round table and two chairs. The stone floor was covered with a, thick, plush carpet that was soft underfoot.

Warm rugs were often used in the interiors of ancient castles; they added a sense of comfort and retained heat. The climate of northern Scotland was harsh, and the close proximity to the North Sea brought cold winds and dampness. However, thanks to modern technology, the McKenzie castle was well-equipped to combat these elements.

"Thank you, Gregor, everything is perfect. I'll see you tomorrow at ten."

"The meeting hall is to the right of the main entrance on the ground floor. Have a good evening, Miss."

"Megan, if you have no further questions for me, I'll take my leave as well."

"No questions, Mr. Douglas, thank you for meeting me. I'm very grateful."

2
Independent Life

She didn't know how long she would need to stay in Scotland, so she packed enough for a stay of about two to three weeks. She could manage her time freely, as back in London, her romance with a young man had ended, and the restaurant her mother had opened sixteen years ago was in excellent hands with a great manager.

After Arline moved to America, the business was left to Megan. She was only eleven when she started taking an interest in her mother's work. She saw how Arline loved her business and was proud of it. Megan, too, wanted to experience the same joy as her mom and emulate her in every way. She spent all her time after school in the restaurant, and over time, began to undergo professional training for future business opportunities. By seventeen, she knew everything about the industry.

Megan was shocked when Arline announced that she was marrying Ted from California and moving to the USA.

"But the restaurant, Mom, what about our restaurant? Surely, you aren't ready to sell something that we've put so much love and effort into over these years?" pleaded Megan desperately.

Arline cried and answered, "Baby, I know it's a very difficult choice right now, but one day you'll understand me. There's nothing more powerful in life than love. When it comes — everything changes: your values and meaning of being. Megan, we'll have a new business in the States and start afresh, bringing all our habits and way of life there. You'll make many new friends, and we'll be happy, all of us together: you, me, and Ted."

"Mom, dear, your values may have changed, but mine haven't. I love this city, this country, this life, and most importantly, this restaurant — not some other. I want to live and work here. Please, don't make me give it up."

At that young age, the girl didn't fully understand what love and a beloved person meant to her mother. They had always been together, working and relaxing in unison. Arline had never been married; she dedicated her entire life to her dearest daughter, and only child.

"Honey, what should we do then? How can I live like this? My soul is torn between two fires: you, my daughter, and him, the love of my life!" the desperate woman sat down in the chair and began to cry bitterly.

Megan's heart was breaking for her mother. *I'm so selfish*, she chided herself.

"Go to America, get married, be happy. I will stay here and run the restaurant. I'm old and mature enough already," she said, making the only decision she felt was right.

"But how will you manage alone? You still need to complete your studies. Have you got any idea how difficult this will be?" said Arline anxiously, worried about her precious daughter.

"I don't think it will be too hard because I love this job. Besides, I'm not alone. We have a good manager; he will help me."

"I will be happy if you succeed. I believe in you; you are a great girl. You take after your grandfather in character, just as stubborn, goal-oriented, and independent. Once you've made up your mind, no one can persuade you otherwise. I'm proud of you, my dear," Arline wiped her tears and hugged her brave daughter tightly.

"Thanks, Mom. I love you. Go in peace and be happy."

"Promise me that if you need any advice, no matter what it is, no matter what time of day or night, you'll call me, and I'll always be ready to help you."

"Of course!"

"I love you, baby!"

"And I love you, Mom!"

Five months after that conversation, Arline got married and moved to California. Over time, Megan realized that her ideas about independent living didn't quite match reality. Due to her perfectionism, she demanded the utmost attention to detail in everything she did. Sleepless nights were spent with textbooks, and days at work. Vacation remained a distant dream, and there was absolutely no time left for a personal life. But she bravely carried on, telling no one just how hard it really was for her.

When Malcolm McKenzie learned during one of his visits that his granddaughter had been living alone and managing the restaurant by herself for a year, he was beside himself with rage. He yelled, unable to contain his anger.

"Your mother was a frivolous girl twenty years ago, and she hasn't matured one bit since. To imagine, abandoning her child, her only daughter, for a man. How dare she, the shameless woman?! Look at you, all skin and bones! Dark circles under your eyes! You're still just a child, but everything has fallen on your frail shoulders! When I die, she won't see a penny of the inheritance. Never will I permit the fortune of our clan to be squandered in another country, and for our family name to be scattered in the wind and forgotten as if it had never existed. You are my pride and joy, Megan. Proud that you stayed and didn't trade Great Britain for another continent."

This conversation had taken place five years prior, and Malcolm has since been visiting his granddaughter in London every year.

Eight months ago, on his last visit, he said, "My health is not what it used to be, Megan. In all likelihood, this is probably my last visit. Now it's your turn to come and visit your old man."

"I was planning to do so this year, but you see, mom had surgery, and I needed to be with her in California. Next summer I will come to visit you for a few weeks. The summer there, as I've heard is the only time of year when you don't freeze to death and drown in the rain," Megan laughed. "But I promise; this time I will definitely come; nothing will make me change my mind."

"Drown in the rain? What nonsense! No doubt your good-for-nothing mother planted such ideas in your head. Of course, it's cooler in the north than in the center of the country, but it's not nearly as awful as you say! Your visit will give me great pleasure. I will arrange a celebration to mark this day."

3

Bagpipes

And now she was here. He would have been so glad to see her. What cause for celebration her arrival might have been. But, as it turned out, she arrived the day after his funeral. He had passed in the evening, and the very next day his body was buried in the McKenzie family crypt, such were the burial customs in this place. Feelings of guilt had tormented her ever since she learned of his death.

"Grandpa, I'm so sorry. Forgive me, please. I didn't make it in time," she whispered. Wiping away the tears streaming down her cheeks, the girl thought that she couldn't permit herself to break down right now, she needed a clear head to make important decisions. Tomorrow would be a difficult day and she had to be ready. She would have to meet her grandfather's brother Alaric and his grandchildren, Warren and Duncan. As she recalled from Malcolm's stories, by the twentieth century, their family had two castles in possession: Castle Mal and Castle Raven. Castle Mal was the ancestral home built by the McKenzies, and Castle Raven was inherited from the neighboring Drummond clan in 1898, when the last member disappeared without leaving any heirs. Grandfather Malcolm and Great-Uncle Alaric were the two heirs of David McKenzie, who bequeathed to Alaric, Castle Raven and the wool factory, while Malcolm inherited Castle Mal and the Scotch whisky distillery. At present, Alaric and Duncan are residing at Castle Raven, while Warren and his wife are temporarily staying at Castle Mal with Megan, who, from tomorrow, will become the official owner of the ancestral home, after the lawyer reads the will. The best solution that came to Megan's mind was to offer the relatives to buy the distillery and the castle from her, if they so wished. She had no intention of selling the estate to strangers; she didn't want Malcolm turning over in his grave, knowing that the clan's home had been sold to someone outside the family circle.

Having changed her clothes and finished unpacking, Megan looked at the clock on the fireplace mantel. What a long day it had been; the memories of arriving at the airport that morning felt as if they were a week old. The clock showed 22:25. The room was getting cooler, and turning on the heater, she draped a shawl over her shoulders. She was about to go and remove her make-up when she heard an unusual sound. It took her a while to figure out where it was coming from. She listened carefully. This intriguing continuous melody was mesmerizing, capturing her attention and evoking a vague sense of unease.

"Bagpipes," she said softly.

Her heart suddenly pounded loudly, while her soul clenched sweetly yet painfully. The girl couldn't understand why the sounds of a Scottish musical instrument stirred her so deeply. It was as if something magical, something supernatural, was beckoning her. She opened the window and saw that someone was playing the bagpipes not far from the castle. After listening for a short while, Megan left her room, drawn to stand outside and savor the melody. Leaving the house, she struggled to make out the shapes of objects until her eyes adjusted to the darkness. It was cool outside; the temperature had dropped and the wind from the sea sent chills down her spine.

Within a few minutes, she could clearly see the river at the base of the castle grounds, and hear the North Sea's rumble to her right. The sound of the bagpipes came from that direction. There was no one around, but she wasn't afraid. It was strange; she never made such reckless decisions, always cautious of the dark, but this time, she was magnetically drawn towards the source of the magical music. She walked as if enchanted. The area was private property and unlikely accessible to just anyone. With such thoughts, she calmed herself, rationalizing her impetuous act. She knew the entrance to the castle was nearby, and if fear overtook her, she could quickly return.

At that moment, the full moon came to her aid, appearing in the sky and illuminating the river and surrounding hills. On one of the hilltops, Megan noticed a man with a bagpipe. His tall, graceful figure resembled one of the true northern highlanders described in legends. He stood with his legs shoulder-width apart, wearing a Scottish kilt and high white woolen socks up to his knees. Megan couldn't make out the colors of the kilt, the moonlight wasn't bright enough to illuminate the details. The jacket, with a cape, was draped over his left shoulder. He continued playing the same heartbreaking melody, which was as beautiful as it was sad. Megan crept forwards, desperately wanting to take a closer look at him, to fulfill her irresistible desire. Her soul trembled as if her life depended on the encounter with this highlander. But the moon hid behind a cloud as suddenly as it had appeared, and the melody stopped.

It became very dark, and only the sound of the sea was audible. Megan felt an instant sense of unease, as if she had just awoken from a dream. Despite her attempts to discern the stranger's silhouette on the hill, she could not. At that moment, a crunch on the gravel came from behind. She froze in place, feeling as though someone was watching her. But there was no one around.

You're just tired, Megan soothed herself mentally, that's why you're seeing things.

But her heart was racing with fear. She had decided to return to the castle when she heard another sound, a rustling. The girl quickly turned and saw the shadow in a black cloak. It was following her. A soul-chilling fear paralyzed Megan. Somehow, she knew this was not the highlander with bagpipes, it was someone else.

The man in a cloak, with a hood thrown over his head, began to approach Megan, putting a finger to his lips, gesturing for her to be silent. Something ominous emanated from him; his intentions were clearly the most terrifying imaginable, she felt it with every cell in her body. The girl backed away, and in a state of fright, she didn't immediately realize that her feet were in the water; she didn't feel the cold of the river. Panic took over completely, and she dashed towards the entrance door. It was only about thirty meters away. The shadow moved along the shore, thereby blocking the path to the castle entrance.

"Gregor, help!" Megan screamed. She heard the man approaching, turned to see how close he was, and stumbling, fell backwards, hitting her head on a river rock. She didn't even have time to feel the pain. All her thoughts were focused on one thing — survival. Frantically moving, she unsuccessfully tried to get up. Fear increasingly immobilized her movements. Meanwhile, the moon emerged from behind the clouds, illuminating everything once again, including the figure in the black cloak whose face was not visible. Suddenly, the flash of a blade of knife raised above her head. A rush of adrenalin gave the girl a little strength. She managed to crawl slightly away from the attacker, and just at that moment, a loud bird cry suddenly pierced the night. A huge, as Megan perceived, black raven flew directly at the face of the potential killer. The assailant swung the knife towards it but missed; the raven was more agile, hitting the face and head of the wrongdoer with its claws and wings. The attacker, trying to fend off the bird, dropped the knife and attempted to grab it by the wings, but in vain. Finally losing his balance, he fell on the riverbank, rolled onto his stomach, and covered his head with his hands, fearing the raven would peck out his eyes. After a minute, the assailant jumped to his feet and, bending over double to protect his face, ran away from the scene. Megan watched everything as if in a dream. Whether from the shock she had experienced or from the blow to her skull, her vision darkened, and she lost consciousness, never knowing how the struggle ended.

4
Heather

When Megan awoke, she didn't immediately realize where she was. In all certainty, she was lying in bed. The girl turned her head. The mantel clock showed 7:40. The sun was shining through the windows. Reconstructing the events from the previous night in her mind, she reached the moment when she heard the sound of the bagpipes and went outside. It took her breath away. Could everything that followed really be true? Or was it a dream? Just a terrible nightmare? Sitting up in bed, she took a careful look at herself. She was wearing the same clothes as the previous day. In the evening, she had put on white trousers, which were now completely soiled. Her beige and-white blouse was covered in mud, she had no shoes on her feet, and on the side of the bed lay her beige stole, all crumpled and wet.

"My God! It wasn't a dream! How did I end up here? Who brought me back to my room?" Megan whispered in horror. Gregor? Warren? What happened to the man who tried to kill me? Could she have ever imagined that the trip to her ancestral home would turn out to be so dangerous?! After all, she hadn't even left the castle grounds.

Slowly getting out of bed, Megan went to the bathroom to clean herself up before meeting her relatives. Moreover, she was eager to see Gregor and find out what had happened after she lost consciousness.

*****

Megan put on a formal black suit and low-heeled shoes, pulled her thick chestnut-brown hair into a bun, and finished off with a few light and subtle touches of makeup. She descended the wide staircase into the hall. Terrifying memories crowded in again, scenes of what she had experienced flashed through her mind like a movie. There she was, walking to the front door, mesmerized by the music, leaving the castle…

I wonder, what role the highlander with the bagpipes had to play in all this? From his vantage point on the hill, he must have had a clear view of what was happening on the riverbank. But he didn't come to help. Perhaps he was in league with the attacker?

Megan looked around. The castle was dead silent as if she were completely alone. Suddenly, the estate manager appeared, as if from nowhere.

"Oh, Gregor, I was looking for you," she said anxiously.

"Good morning, Miss. What can I do for you? Are you comfortable in your room?"

"Yes, quite. I left the castle last night. I heard the bagpipes and wanted to find out who was playing…" she paused, waiting for a reaction to her words.

"The bagpipes?" Gregor asked, surprised. "I didn't hear anything like that."

"You didn't leave the castle at all yesterday evening?"

"No, Miss, I didn't. After I left your room, I worked for several hours on the reports for our gathering today."

"I see. Thank you," the girl took a brief pause. "Where is the kitchen? I'd like to have breakfast before meeting my relatives."

"The assembly hall is to the right of the stairs, and the kitchen is opposite it."

"Thank you."

"See you later, Miss."

Megan was frantically pondering who had brought her to the bedroom after the night's incident, if not Gregor. Could he be the one in the black cloak? He hadn't heard the bagpipes nor responded to her scream. Could there be a conspiracy against her? Or was it truly a maniac who didn't care whom he killed?

Utmost caution is necessary; trusting anyone is now out of the question. Anybody could be the enemy. Yet, what reason would Gregor have to kill me? What would he gain from it? My relatives could be involved, considering their potential interest in the inheritance.

Her mind was a whirlwind of confusion, ideas buzzing like a swarm of bees. The question of who had brought her into the castle at night haunted the girl. This person somehow knew which bedroom she was staying in. Lost in deep thought, she entered the kitchen. At the head of the table, was a man not much older than Megan, with hair the same color as hers, well-built and quite attractive. His face looked a bit tired. To his right sat a woman who appeared to be near Megan in age. Her light brown hair was pulled back in a tight bun, and she was wearing practically no makeup, yet her face was open and pleasant enough. They sat in silence, drinking tea, and seemed quite contemplative.

These were Warren and his wife. Her grandfather had mentioned that the cousins were a couple of years older than her, but Megan couldn't recall their exact age. Seeing her, the man quickly put his cup down and stood up with a polite smile.

"Hello, I'm Warren, and this is my wife, Glenn. Malcolm spoke a lot about you, always in good terms," he said.

"Good morning. It's nice to meet you," replied Megan, with a slightly strained smile.

"Please, have a seat," offered Glenn, pushing warm croissants towards her and pouring a cup of hot tea. Megan felt that the woman seemed slightly embarrassed when their eyes met.

"Thank you. We didn't have a chance to meet yesterday; did you come back late?" Megan asked, hoping that her relatives could shed some light on the evening's events.

"Yes, we got back well after midnight," Warren responded. "There was a tragedy in Glenn's family, and we had to go to Inverness. My apologies we were unable to meet you."

"It's fine, Mr. Douglas and Gregor helped me."

"Megan, Malcolm felt very lonely before he passed, and asked us to stay with him. I think it would be proper for Glenn and me to return to Castle Raven after today's meeting," the cousin seemed to justify his presence in the castle.

"As you wish, but if you decide to stay a bit longer, I'd be glad. It would give us a chance to get to know each other better." The thought of staying alone in this large, cold castle, aside from Gregor, terrified her.

"Alright," Warren smiled more warmly this time, "we'll stay a few more days and help you get accustomed to the place."

"Great, thank you," said Megan. She thought to herself: First of all, it wasn't Warren who brought me in last night. Most likely it was the Highlander with the bagpipes. But why would he do this, and how did he know which bedroom was mine? Time will sort things out. But it would be best to wrap up the business here as quickly as possible and head back to London.

Having finished their tea, they all went to the assembly hall together. Its stone walls were adorned with deer antlers and other hunting trophies. A massive mahogany table was placed in the center. Lancet windows along the long wall made the hall very bright, offering a beautiful view of the river and hills.

Mr. Douglas, Gregor, and two men unknown to Megan, were already seated at the table. The eldest of them stood up when she entered.

"Hello Megan. It's my pleasure to welcome you to your historic homeland. My brother had been dreaming of your arrival for years, and now that day has finally come. I am Alaric McKenzie, your late grandfather's brother."

His words made the girl feel guilty, as they sounded like a reproach, but she kept her emotions in check and calmly replied that the pleasure was mutual.

"Hi, I'm Duncan," said the other man, grinning broadly and gazing at her admiringly. "What a pity that we're related by blood; otherwise, I'd have already started courting you." The cousin not only shook her hand but also kissed her on both cheeks as if they were old friends who hadn't seen one another in years.

Duncan was a bit taller than Warren. A good-looking figure, playful eyes — everything about him suggested that he was a very confident young man and had no shortage of women. When he smiled, his handsome face radiated incredible magnetism. If Warren gave the impression of a very serious and modest person, Duncan was the complete opposite: cheerful, lively, uninhibited, he immediately became the center of attention. It seemed that energy was bursting out of him like a fountain.

Megan was pleasantly surprised to find all her relatives — dressed in traditional style. Each wore a woolen kilt in clan colors, still an integral part of the Scottish national costume. The men's skirts with large pleats at the back; a tartan plaid thrown over the left shoulder, secured with a brooch. A white shirt, handkerchief tie, black waistcoat, and black jacket – all perfectly fit the members of the McKenzie family. High woolen socks up to the knees, and over the belt hung a sporran — a leather pouch on a chain that fastened around the waist. It featured three small, rabbit tail-like attachments.

Carefully observing all this magnificence, the girl thought that the male members of the McKenzie family were very distinguished by their tall stature and good physiques. Aloud, she remarked, "I've seen many Scots in national dress in England, including Grandfather, but never paid attention to the details. It's truly very beautiful and extraordinarily elegant, especially when men know how to handle all the accompanying accessories, which, I think, many people these days neglect. All three of you look gorgeous — like Scottish national fashion models."

"You are absolutely correct. A properly assembled costume is our history, which started here in these mountains, and we are proud of our traditions. In the big towns, few people nowadays wear kilts; they mostly prefer trousers. But the northern Scots will never abandon their customs."

Having delivered his speech on national attire, Alaric took his place at the head of the table. His grandsons, Duncan and Warren, sat beside him. Megan noted how much Alaric and her grandfather resembled each other. A robust, gray-haired man, shorter than his grandsons, with a serious expression on his face. The eyes, nose, authoritative chin, were all so reminiscent of Malcolm... It felt as if they were of the same age. This resemblance poignantly touched her soul. The whole family was here, but he was not...

She couldn't remember who was actually older, Alaric or Malcolm. Presumably, it was Grandfather since he had inherited Castle Mal, the ancestral home of the clan.

"Mr. Douglas, you may begin," Warren said.

"All the members of the McKenzie family are gathered here today for the reading of the will of the late Malcolm

McKenzie," Mr. Douglas began. "Allow me to state his will: 'I hereby bequeath Castle Mal and the Mal Scotch Production whisky distillery, as well as all the funds remaining in my bank accounts, to my only granddaughter, Megan McKenzie.' Miss McKenzie, there is one more amendment you should be aware of. In the event of your death, if there are no legitimate children-heirs, your mother cannot inherit what your grandfather left you. The entire estate will pass to Alaric and his grandsons, as was the deceased's wish," concluded Mr. Douglas.

Following these words, Megan was frantically thinking. It must be one of them trying to kill me, now it all makes sense. If I'm gone, they are the lawful heirs. This means another attempt on my life is imminent. Oh, what a nightmare! What should I do? There's no point in offering the family to buy the estate now. Why would they spend the money if they can get it all for free?

After several seconds of complete silence, Alaric asked her a question, "Megan, how are you going to manage the distillery and the castle? Are you going to stay in Scotland, or would you like to manage things from London?"

"This is precisely why I came here — to see the distillery first-hand and get acquainted with its management specifics. Based on this, I will make my decision. Perhaps you have some thoughts on this matter?"

"We can offer our assistance if you find it challenging. I believe Warren wouldn't mind looking after the castle, and along with Gregor, managing the production. Duncan is involved with our other factory with its woolen products. Warren is more available time-wise. As for the terms of your cooperation, I believe you are capable of negotiating them if you're interested in such an arrangement."

"Thank you, Alaric. I will certainly consider your offer," trying to speak very calmly and without unnecessary emotions, Megan continued, "but... there's something I'd like to discuss. Last night, near the castle, I was attacked by a man with a knife. He tried to kill me. I don't want to accuse anyone of what happened, but just in case, I'm informing you that due to the inheritance order that has been revealed to me, I will definitely, right after the meeting, call my lawyer in London and ask him to prepare a document. If something happens to me, a thorough investigation will be conducted based on the information about a possible direct interest in inheritance matters."

The meeting room fell into complete silence, surprised looks turned into offended ones. Duncan was the first to recover and find a voice to speak.

"Megan, what are you saying! You just arrived here, you're meeting us for the first time, you've got no idea what kind of people we are, and you start threatening us? I can't speak for my grandfather and brother, but personally, I'm offended to the core," his cheerfulness and friendliness were abruptly replaced by a kind of aggression. His cousin's statement seriously angered him.

"I had no intention of offending or insulting anyone here. But since an attempt was made on my life yesterday, I think it's quite reasonable that I bring this up — since I obviously have good reason to fear."

"I'm terribly sorry that this happened to you, but it's hard to imagine. Could it have been some drunkard attacking you with the intention of robbery? It might just be a coincidence," said Alaric in bewilderment.

"This man was following me and attacked me with a knife, but…" Megan hesitated for a moment, reluctant to mention the raven, knowing it would sound ridiculous, "but I swiftly dodged him. He slipped on some rocks near the riverbank and fell. That saved me, and I managed to escape."

Everyone in the assembly hall exchanged puzzled looks. Who could it be? Why and for what reason? No one had answers to these questions, and it seemed unlikely that the girl had made up this story.

The awkward silence was broken by Gregor, "Miss McKenzie, I've prepared all the accounting reports for you; they're in this folder. You can review them whenever you deem necessary. I am ready to answer any questions you may have."

"Thank you, Gregor. I'll start on them today," she replied.

"Since Megan does not yet have any ideas regarding the future of Castle Mal and the distillery, we should schedule another meeting in the near future. What do you say, Megan? How much time do you need? A week, two?" asked Alaric.

"I think we should discuss everything in about ten days. I need to study the documents carefully and make an informed decision," she answered.

"Despite the unfortunate situation we find ourselves in today, on behalf of our family, I still invite you to join us for dinner this Friday at Castle Raven. I believe we all need to get to know each other better. We are still one family, after all. Maybe you will stop fearing and suspecting us," said Alaric more warmly, but still a bit stiffly.

"We'll be glad to have you as our guest," added Duncan, now composed, with a restrained, polite smile.

"Thank you, I will come. Is it far from here?"

"A ten-minute walk up the hill behind Castle Mal. Glenn and I will escort you," Warren replied.

"I would greatly appreciate that. Alaric, Duncan, it was nice meeting you. I'll go study the materials now," saying this, the girl quickly left.

What a foolish situation. They offered help, seemed friendly, and here I am with accusations, threats... Such absurdity. But on the other hand, they could be pretending. It might be a cunningly planned game. Time will tell. I shouldn't torment myself with guilt over what I said there. At least, now everyone knows about the attempt on my life. She thought while walking through the castle's corridor.

Megan really wanted to visit the family crypt where her grandfather now rested. Before the meeting started, she had planned to ask her relatives to accompany her there since she was afraid to go alone. But given how things turned, she felt it was improper to ask any of them now. Before delving into the documents, she decided to take a short walk, familiarize herself with the surroundings, and organize her thoughts. The weather was splendid, with the temperature reaching twenty degrees Celsius, quite warm for the north of Scotland.

Walking toward the shore, she relished the warm summer sun caressing her face. Just to be safe, she looked around carefully to make sure no one was following her. There was nobody in sight. It took her about ten or fifteen minutes to reach the beach through the green-pink meadows.

Gazing at the horizon and admiring the sea, she didn't immediately understand what had startled her so abruptly. Megan looked around again — nobody was there. Then she realized it was a bird. A large black raven had flown over her head two or three times with a cry. She feared it was the same one from her nightmare, worried it might attack her face as it had done with the assailant. But the bird flew off towards a cliff. Perching on an outcrop, it continued to watch the girl unblinkingly. She too could not take her eyes off it for several minutes, then shifted her gaze back to the water. Megan didn't know how long she had spent walking along the beach in contemplation. An hour, two? The raven remained on the same spot, watching her intently. Soon, she stopped paying it any attention and headed back to the castle.

So much heather around, covering all the hills, fields, mountains, just as grandfather described. Now I understand those who say the most picturesque part of Scotland is the north. Could it be that my mother never wished to come back here again? To once more enjoy the beauty so generously bestowed upon this land by nature.

Megan's contemplations were abruptly interrupted by a voice, "In the North of Scotland, heather is considered a flower of happiness and good luck."

Startled, the girl almost jumped on the spot, fearfully placing her hand over her mouth to suppress a slight scream. She had been so absorbed in her thoughts that she hadn't noticed the old lady who had stopped beside her, holding a straw basket filled with heather. She held out one of the flowering sprigs to Megan.

"Oh God, you scared me," said Megan.

The woman appeared to be about 85 years old. Short in stature, slightly stooped as if weighed down by the years she had lived, her snow-white hair was neatly tied back. Wrinkles furrowed her forehead, around her eyes, and lips, betraying her advanced age, while her bluish-grey eyes radiated wisdom and kindness.

"Take a flower, my dear; it brings luck. Who knows, maybe you will find the happiness left behind in the distant past…"

"Thank you," the girl replied, accepting the flower.

She didn't understand what kind of lost happiness the woman was talking about. Maybe it was about her mother leaving the family home while pregnant. Or perhaps the old lady had just lost her mind…

"What's your name?"

"Innes Wallace, and you're Megan McKenzie, the late Malcolm's granddaughter. It's good that you've come back. The time has come. He has been waiting for you for so long, it's time, it's time, he has waited… May the pink heather stand in your room every day. You will see how you will regain your lost happiness. You'll see; you'll see. Love overcomes all, even centuries cannot diminish its power…"

With these words, Innes moved further away. Meanwhile, she continued to mutter to herself, seemingly forgetting about the existence of the girl watching her in astonishment.

"What was that?" Megan whispered quietly.

Concluding that the woman was out of her mind and didn't understand what she was talking about, Megan decided to take the flower to her bedroom. Let it stay, maybe it really will bring good luck. I need it now more than ever!

The rest of the day, the girl spent exploring the castle from the inside, and only in the evening did she start reviewing the reports given by Gregor. Tomorrow, she intended to visit the distillery and acquaint herself with the production processes.

Preparing for bed, Megan heard again the heart-wrenching sounds of the bagpipes. It was 10.45 p.m. on the mantel clock. Pain and sweetness filled her soul at the same time. The melody was enticing, mesmerizing, but the girl was afraid to leave her room. If it was a trap, she could be attacked again… She opened the window and saw the mysterious stranger. The moonlight illuminated him well. He stood on the same hill as the night before. The man raised his head so he could look at her, without stopping the musical instrument. Megan's breath was taken away, and a thought flashed through her mind, It's him. Tears welled up in her eyes. Her hands and legs trembled so much that she was afraid to fall. Not understanding what was happening to her, the girl whispered, "Who is he?" An inner voice answered, "It's him." But who "he" was remained unclear.

Emotions swept over her one after another: sadness, pain, love, despair, joy. Megan couldn't make out the stranger's features, but she knew for sure that his face was the most beautiful in the world, that the scent of his skin, his body, was the most desirable to her in the world. The highlander kept playing the bagpipes without taking his eyes off the girl. It seemed to Megan that he saw right through her, reading her thoughts and feelings. With an incredible effort of will, she forced herself to close the window, shivering as if from cold, although the room was warm.

"My God! What's happening to me? What kind of obsession is this?"

Without turning back to the view of the hills, the girl went to bed, but for a long time she could still hear the sad melody of the Scottish bagpipes, and she was unable to calm the feverish excitement that flooded her soul.

When Megan looked at the clock for the last time, it was already four in the morning. Falling into a restless sleep, she saw the highlander next to her bedside, whispering to her, "I've been waiting for you, Megan." He kissed her tenderly and then disappeared, jumping outside, into the darkness.

She woke up late, a bit after 10 a.m. There was a fresh scent in the room — the smell of grass and nature.

"Nature! Grass!" Megan jumped up in bed, realizing that the window, through which the stranger disappeared in her dream, was wide open. The girl tried to recall closing it the night before but couldn't; she'd been too excited.

"I simply forgot to close it yesterday," she convinced herself to calm down. "It's just a coincidence. My nerves are frayed from stress. My God, what's been happening to me these past few days? Complete madness!"

5

Scotch Whisky

When Megan descended the staircase, she saw that Warren and Gregor were already waiting for her in the hall.

"Good morning," greeted the girl.

"Good morning," the men said in unison.

"Have you had breakfast yet?" her cousin inquired.

"No, I was just about to have a cup of coffee now. I didn't think you'd be ready before the appointed time."

"It's all right, Megan, no need to rush. We've got plenty of time."

She quickly went to the kitchen. In two minutes, she managed to drink coffee and eat a small piece of shortbread. Megan didn't like being late and felt uncomfortable if she kept someone waiting. Punctuality and perfectionism were in her blood. Brushing the biscuit crumbs off her fingers, she hurried back to the hall.

After leaving the castle, they got into Warren's car and Megan asked how far it was to the distillery.

"We'll be there in ten minutes," he replied.

"Warren, would you be able to take me to the family crypt afterwards? I'd like to pay my final respects to Grandfather, but I don't dare go there alone. It's a bit creepy." She felt very awkward asking for anything after the unpleasant situation the day before, which she herself had created. But there was no choice; she had to establish a rapport between them.

"Yes, of course, as soon as we return, we'll go there."

"Thanks a lot."

"Megan, if there's anything I can do for you, don't hesitate to ask. I'm always ready to help."

The girl nodded in appreciation and said, "Tell me, are there any other inhabited castles around here besides Castle Raven and Castle Mal?"

"In the nearest thirty miles, definitely not. However, there are some abandoned ones that hold historical value for tourists. There are many such places throughout Scotland."

"Don't you find it boring living here all the time?"

"Not at all. We're used to a measured way of life. I don't know anyone who could get bored with a such beautiful place. We don't stay locked up at home for weeks. We work, have fun, hunt. There are a lot of deer, wild boars, and hares in the local forests. It's a true pleasure. We, Highlanders, really love our local, traditional festivals, and they happen quite often. I hope you get to attend such an event. The next one is in four days. It's called the Witch's Night, or Fern Night. According to Celtic beliefs, it's the only night of the year when you can see the fern flower bloom. It lasts only a moment. It's very difficult to pick the flower, especially since evil forces do everything to prevent it, sometimes even driving people to madness."

"I've never heard in my life that ferns could bloom," Megan exclaimed in surprise, looking at Warren with wide eyes, trying not to miss a word of his story.

"The fern flower is mythical, supposedly revealing the secrets of the magical world to its owner. It also grants clairvoyance and power over evil spirits. Evil forces try in every way to distract the hunter, for example, by calling out to him with the voice of a loved one. And if one turns around at the call, it could cost them their life. It means looking into the eyes of death."

"That's terrifying! Do locals really believe in this to this day?"

"Of course, Megan. You can't imagine how many people head off into the bracken before midnight. Each one of them hopes that they will be the lucky one. Some even go into the forest!"

"Do you know at least one person who has actually had such luck?"

"Not yet," laughed Warren. "But my grandfather knows many legends related to it. He believes in the fern flower bloom, as do many of his age. They say that in the past, most northern Highlanders had abilities for clairvoyance, witchcraft, and so on. Our land is special, and so are the people here. Well, I'm skeptical about it, but my wife, Glenn, believes everything my grandfather and his peers tell her. If you're interested," he continued with a smile, "she can tell you a lot more. I, for one, love this festival like the others, simply because the whole north celebrates. Our people have fun, dance and play the bagpipes. Ale, cider, whisky, flow like rivers. Various Northern Scottish dishes are available to choose from. Lots of local game. Meat that's cured, grilled on coals, pan-fried, stewed, and anything else you could want. Almost all the townspeople and neighboring villagers come here. After all, the forest is nearby, and most ferns grow near us too. Tents, wooden tables, and benches are set up on the hill."

"Warren! It sounds wonderful! I can't wait for this festival!"

"We Highlanders just need an excuse to have fun! Well, Megan, here we are."

"Thank you. Your story was absolutely fascinating. If you and Glenn have got time this evening, I would love to hear more legends related to the traditions of Northern Scotland."

"Of course! Tonight, after dinner, we'll happily share with you all we know about our north over a glass of whisky by the fireplace."

"Great, I'm already looking forward to it," Megan spoke joyously, pleased with Warren's openness and the fact that he harbored no resentment toward her for the previous day's events.

When Megan got out of the car, she found herself in front of a long two-story building made of large stone blocks. This style, she noted, was a common feature of most historical buildings in Scotland. The distillery was situated on a hill. From there, magnificent landscapes opened up. Megan thought it would be impossible to get used to such beauty. Surely, these views could never become dull.

"How long has this distillery been here?" she asked her cousin.

"From the 15th century. It was built by our ancestor William McKenzie, in 1486. Naturally, a lot has changed and improved inside since then. But externally, it remains as it was centuries ago."

At the entrance to the building, a large oak barrel lay on its side, with "Mal Scotch Production" painted on it in white; the clan coat of arms was underneath.

Gregor, who had come with them but had remained silent the whole way, swung the door open, gesturing for them to enter. The girl immediately noticed a distinctive smell — malt, as it seemed to her.

Megan didn't consider herself an expert in this field. She had never been fond of strong alcoholic beverages, preferring ale or cider instead. She had only drunk whisky once in her life, a few years back, and now barely remembered how it smelled. Inside, there was a reception desk and a small sofa. A pleasant-looking blonde woman — around fifty, dressed in a smart business suit, immediately approached the visitors.

"Good afternoon, Miss McKenzie. My name is Kirsty, I'm the head technologist at the distillery. Warren, Gregor, it's good to see you. If you're ready, we can proceed further. I will take you to the production technology and show you the distillery."

"Thank you, Kirsty; lead the way," Megan said.

In the room where the first stage of production took place, there was a huge vessel.

"This is the mash tun, where barley is added. Then, water is poured into it and left for 4-5 days. This is called the malting stage. During this time, the starch turns into sugar. The barley grains, after this process, need to be thoroughly dried with hot smoke from peat. We do that here," the woman pointed towards an open door to another large room. "The peat subsequently gives the barley a unique aroma, which becomes an integral part of the future whisky."

Moving ahead into the next room, Kirsty showed a massive purpose-built machine designed to grind malt into flour. Next to it was another huge mash vat.

"In this vat," she continued, "we mix the grain with hot water, and keep it for about twelve hours. Then, in the cooled wort, we add yeast for the fermentation process to occur. After that, the contents of the vat are transferred into these copper stills. In there, the heat increases to 86 degrees Celsius. The alcohol rises up through the tubes then cools back down into a liquid state. This process is called distillation. It usually happens twice so that the content reaches 70 degrees. Then, we pour the obtained liquid into oak barrels and send them to the warehouse. The minimum period the liquid must age to be called whisky is three years. During this time, the spirit evaporates from sixty to forty degrees. The longer the whisky stays in the barrel, the richer its color and taste become. Whisky is the water of life, as they say in the north of Scotland."

The small procession moved on, listening to Kirsty.

"And in this room, we proceed to bottling and packaging. As you can see, there is nothing complicated; just barley, water, yeast, and time."

"Are the grain and barrels local?" Megan inquired.

Warren took the liberty in answering this question.

"The best Scottish grain grows here in the north. We have peaty heather fields which are unique to us, giving barley a special flavor. And we order oak barrels from Andalusia, Spain that come with sherry. The best barrels for whisky are those from sherry."

"Thank you! You explained everything in great detail."

They also visited the warehouses where barrels filled with whisky are stored. Megan tasted one of the aged single malt varieties, twenty years in maturation, noting that the flavor was very rich and the alcohol was barely noticeable. "Now I understand what good Scottish whisky means!" she said with a smile.

For another two hours, they remained at the distillery. Gregor and Kirsty educated the new owner on employee work details, explained how many people were involved in the production, and much more.

6
Legends of the North

After going up to her room, Megan sat on the bed and reflected. Too many events had occurred during the three days she had been here. It felt like a whole week had passed since her arrival. Meeting new people who had now become her family; the harsh and majestic beauty of the nature and the castle she was living in; an attempt on her life; visiting her own whiskey distillery... She had experienced so many different impressions and emotions, more than she had ever experienced in London with its fast-paced, event-filled life over a year.

Megan didn't immediately notice the strange rustling at the window. Turning around, she saw a black raven. It sat on the outside windowsill, staring intently at her. The thought that this bird was constantly watching her made her uneasy. Trying to calm herself, she thought that there were probably many such birds in this area.

After resting for a bit, she went down to the hall and waited for her cousin. Soon he appeared and said, "Well, Megan, are you ready?"

"Yes, let's go."

Upon entering the chapel, which was about hundred yards from the castle, Megan admired the ancient structure.

"It's beautiful," she remarked, examining the old building closely.

"Yes, and this chapel remembers all the marriages, baptisms, and funerals of the McKenzie clan. It was built at the same time as the old castle."

Inside, to the left of the altar, there was a massive wrought iron door leading to the family crypt. Warren opened it with a key, and Megan shivered at the realization that the burials were so close to the castle. She feared anything associated with death.

The young people moved down the grim, quiet corridor, passing other doors, but these were not locked. After passing several, they stopped at the penultimate one.

Warren swung it open for his cousin, "Go ahead."

Megan was frightened, feeling as if dozens of eyes were watching her from all sides. She saw a recent burial to the right of the entrance. Unlike the others, it was not covered in dust. Fresh flowers stood in vases at the gravestone. The stone bore the name, birth date, and death date in large letters. It was her grandfather's resting place.

Tears rolled down her cheeks. Only now did she fully comprehend that he was no longer among the living. He would never come to her in London again. He would never call her to Castle Mal. She was already here. She had come, but it seemed Malcolm had to die for his beloved granddaughter to finally be in his homeland. These thoughts made her feel even worse. She whispered to herself, Here I am. You waited. But I can't hug you now, or tell you how much I love you, how much you mean to me, how much I miss you! Forgive me! Forgive my late arrival. You will forever remain in my heart and memory. I love you, Grandpa! I promise to do everything in my power to ensure that everything in our estate goes as you would have wished. I've already grown to love your beloved north and your home with all my heart.

After standing by the grave for another ten minutes, she wiped her tears and said, "Thank you, Warren, for coming here with me. We can return to the castle now."

"As you wish."

Her cousin patted her shoulder sympathetically, and they headed back to the house through the chapel.

"Where is the key to the crypt kept? I would like to come here again to bring flowers to Grandpa."

"In Malcolm's former office. In the drawer of his desk, you'll find the keys to all the doors in the castle."

"Thanks. I'll go to my room. What time shall we meet for dinner?"

"At seven. Is that time convenient for you?"

"Yes, perfect."

Megan spent the next few hours reviewing the documents previously given to her by Gregor. She also called her assistant Sam to check on the restaurant's affairs. He assured her that everything was fine and there was nothing to worry about.

Megan breathed a sigh of relief, it's good to have someone reliable to count on.

*****

When she came down for dinner, Glenn was already busily helping the cook set the table.

"Hi, Megan! Warren said you had a tough day today."

"Yes, it wasn't the easiest. I'm so sorry I didn't make it here earlier while Grandpa was still alive. Things would have been entirely different."

"Don't be so hard on yourself. It's all God's will. It must have been predestined for you to come to us when you did. Finella has prepared stewed lamb with mashed potatoes for dinner tonight. I hope you'll like it. This dish is very popular in the north. Sorry, we didn't ask in advance what kind of meat you prefer."

"I'm not picky about food. I'll be very happy to try the local cuisine. Glenn, I've been meaning to ask, who takes care of the castle and its surroundings?"

"Finella is responsible for preparing lunches and dinners, and she also keeps the dining room clean. Everyone cleans their own room. About once a month, a cleaning company comes to mop the floors, clean the walls and carpets; basically, do a deep clean of the whole house. When needed, we call the gardener, who has been trimming our lawns and bushes for many years. Malcolm used to take care of everything. Now it's our responsibility."

Over dinner, they discussed production matters, and Warren explained his management duties. Megan replied that his responsibilities would now increase and so would his earnings accordingly.

Towards the end of the meal, Glenn turned to the cousin of her husband, "Warren mentioned you're interested in the traditions and legends of our area. We'd be delighted to share everything we know about it with you."

"And I'll be delighted to hear it!"

"Then we can move to the living room, and over a glass of whisky, begin our stories, which you've been anticipating like little girls. Oh, ladies, how you love fairy tales!" Warren said with a playful smile.

Megan took a seat on the sofa. The couple settled into armchairs by the fireplace, where logs softly crackled, adding warmth to the large room.

"There are no ghosts in the castle, right?" Megan asked cautiously.

Warren laughed and replied, "I've never encountered any, and Malcolm never mentioned any to me. So, I can assure you, there have been no ghosts here for at least the last seventy years. And you, I see, are quite the scaredy-cat. Afraid of everything."

"Well, not everything, just inexplicable things: the darkness, and the dead."

"You should be afraid of the living, not the dead! Inexplicable things are always explainable, depending on how you look at it. The dead, they're sleeping peacefully and not making any trouble. Why do you have this fear? Did something happen in the past?"

"No, thank God! And hopefully, it never will. Perhaps, as a child, my friends and I told each other too many horror stories, and I was impressionable. Or, for example, that one movie about Freddy Krueger was enough. Left me scarred for life," Megan said, laughing.

"So, maybe we shouldn't talk about legends today? They're all related to something, as you say, inexplicable."

"No, no, Warren, it's different! This is about the history and traditions of your land. I really want to learn about them to understand what the local people believe in and how they live."

Glenn spoke enthusiastically, "Scots, like many people closely connected with nature, are superstitious. They place great importance on omens, legends, and myths. We celebrate the start and end of the harvest, as well as honoring various saints. Many of the festivals and traditions in northern Scotland are inherited from the Celts. The nearest local one, as Warren already told you, is in four days. On Fern Night, witches' powers are enhanced so, — the most potent magic is performed, and it's the only night it can be undone. It's the most magical and mystical festival we have. And the next one after that is on the first of August. People wear masquerade costumes for it."

"So, on that day, Scots are willing to forsake their beloved traditional attire? By the way, I've noticed that in daily life everyone wears it around here; even the men working at the distillery today were all wearing kilts."

"Our traditions have been in our blood for a very long time," began Warren. "Back in the early medieval era, the highlanders wrapped themselves in dense woolen cloth that protected them from the winds and cold of this region. They would wrap a large plaid around their waist and throw the remaining part over the shoulder and secure it. It was not only convenient and warm for walking but also for sleeping. This was especially appreciated by warriors who had to spend nights under the open sky. During battles, if the costume got in the way, they could easily throw it off with one hand and rush into battle in their birthday suits."

"Are you joking?" laughed Megan.

"I'm not joking, it's true! Often in those times, highlanders fought naked because it was inconvenient to fight in clothes," Warren said enthusiastically.

"What a sight! I can just imagine."

"Over time, the costume evolved, and the kilt became a separate piece. It's still wrapped around the waist, fastened with buckles on the side, and a kilt pin at the bottom," continued the cousin.

Glenn spoke again, "I'm really glad that Scots have preserved their love for the traditional costume and wear it in everyday life. It's truly beautiful. Don't you think so, Megan?"

"I completely agree. I really like it. By the way, I've already seen a man in a kilt playing the bagpipes near the castle in the evening, twice. Is he one of the neighbors?"

Warren raised an eyebrow, "Hmm, possibly. I also heard the melody yesterday. The bagpipe is the main Scottish musical instrument. You can often hear it, but mainly during celebrations or in local pubs. Playing it on the streets, just like that, without any special occasion, is rare."

"At the festival, there will be plenty of bagpipes, and you can fully enjoy the magical music. By the way, legends say that the bagpipes were gifted to the Scots by forest fairies," Glenn replied.

At that moment, Megan was thinking about whether the stranger from the hill would be there. But aloud, she said, "Forest fairies... What other magical creatures are found in these parts?"

"Many people with special abilities have always lived here. For example, old lady Innes, who knows a lot and can see into the future. People from all over the area come to her when traditional medicine doesn't help. Her house stands right next to the forest, like a witch's dwelling. She gathers various herbs for her potions and heals many with infusions and spells. Now, there are almost no people like Innes left, but in the past, the north was full of them. Legends say that the highlanders won many battles thanks to the power of charms and spells."

"They say that in our family, at the end of the nineteenth century, we had a gifted great-great-grandmother, or perhaps some other ancestor. Her name was Margaret McKenzie. She could talk to animals and read their thoughts. She gathered herbs and healed an entire area of diseases. She helped people but only communicated with those in need. She always preferred the company of animals, explaining that they were kinder and more sincere than humans. She was engaged to a lord from a neighboring castle. However, he went missing, and she died of grief, unable to overcome his disappearance. Such a sad story," said Warren.

"Indeed, very sad," Megan replied.

"The castle passed into our possession after the disappearance of Lord Drummond, as he left no heirs and had no relatives. That's Castle Raven, where my grandfather and brother now live. By the way, you remember that we are going there for dinner tomorrow?"

"Yes, I remember. I'm really looking forward to seeing that castle!"

"It's truly extraordinary and looks completely different inside compared to Castle Mal. I think it will make a big impression on you," said Glenn enthusiastically.

"I have no doubt about that. Tell me, Warren, where did Margaret get such a gift? Maybe she picked a fern flower?"

"According to legend, the founder of the clan was Aidan McKenzie. He married a local witch who bewitched him with some kind of love potion. They married despite her having no family or name. From her, along the maternal line, Margaret and a few other females in our clan inherited the gift. However, unlike others who had the ability of clairvoyance, Margaret could only communicate with animals and heal."

"I definitely don't have any gift, which I'm quite happy about," Megan said, laughing.

"Well, that's good. It's probably hard to live with such a thing. To be honest, I don't believe in it. In my opinion, it's just fiction to give a mystical aura to the clan's history and elevate its importance. Maybe Margaret did brew concoctions that actually helped people, but all that can be explained medically. Back then, there weren't many medicines, and she was known as a good doctor and pharmacist, choosing the right herbs for treatment."

"And what about her communication with animals?" asked Glenn to her husband.

"Maybe she fed and trained them... set up a zoo next to the castle. And as for reading thoughts, someone probably embellished that part, and thus a legend was born. Most likely, she was just a regular woman with a talent in medicine and a love for animals."

"And what about the other women in the clan? They had the gift of clairvoyance!" insisted Glenn.

"Perhaps there was only one such person in the clan — Mary. After all, clairvoyants exist all over the world, even today. We only know of Mary McKenzie, who truly had the gift. She lived in the castle from 1632 to 1679. It's said there were others, but no specific names can be given. Mary could see the future and could tell everyone what was, had been, and would be. So, I believe if anyone in our family ever had a magical gift, it was Mary."

Megan, who had been listening to the couple with interest, asked, "And what do your grandfather and brother think, Warren? Do they agree with your opinion?"

"Yes, they also support this version."

Glenn seemed a bit disappointed, "You can think what you like, but I believe in all of it. Megan, will you join us for the fern flower festival?"

"Definitely, I'm eagerly looking forward to the day. But I really hope we won't go searching for the fern flower at midnight. Those are the kinds of things I'm afraid of, even though I don't believe in them, you never know … what if …" the girl answered, laughing.

"Don't worry; we won't be going after the flower. We'll just be enjoying the atmosphere and having fun."

"Great! Warren, Glenn, thank you for taking the time to share all these stories with me; I truly found them very fascinating. To be honest, I didn't expect such warmth and hospitality. My sincerest thanks to you both."

"Come on, Megan! It was our pleasure. As I said earlier today, I hope with time you'll see that we truly are your family and that you can count on us," Warren replied, and Glenn added, "I'm also very glad you're here. Being the only woman among three men, I've been missing having a female friend around. I really hope to find one in you."

"Thank you, Glenn. I think we've already become friends. Overall, I'm very grateful that you both agreed to stay with me for a while. I can't imagine what it would have been like for me alone in such a huge castle."

Megan set aside her empty whiskey glass, wished everyone a good night, and went to her room. In her bedroom, she listened for any sounds, but all was quiet. She approached the window to see if the mysterious man in the kilt was on the hill. It was empty. With a peaceful heart, Megan took a shower and went to bed. Tonight, she was not troubled by irrational thoughts.

7
Sufferings

Despite Megan going to bed without any worries, her night was tormented by nightmares. Margaret, whom Warren had spoken about the day before, sat in a chair by the window in Megan's room, half-turned with her legs pulled up to her chest, crying, and occasionally pressing a handkerchief to her face. She wore a mourning dress, and her black thick hair was spread over her shoulders. The girl's face was in the shadow of the dimmed light.

Then Megan dreamt of the crypt. She was running through its corridors, hearing behind her, "You can't escape from the past." This cry echoed from the tomb where Margaret's remains lay. And at the exit from the crypt, Mary, whom her cousin also mentioned, opened the door for her. She appeared to be about fifty years old and must have been a beautiful woman once. Mary said, "Go, it's still possible to change everything." On a large stone by the chapel sat a black raven, watching Megan. And at the castle's door stood her grandfather Malcolm, who told her, "Thank you for coming, I'm very glad. Now I know you need to be here. It had to happen; the time has come. Mary is right; everything can still be changed. Go forward through life without fear, no matter what and in spite of everything. I will protect you, my girl."

At these words, Megan woke up. It was six-thirty in the morning. Good thing it's light, she thought, or I would have gone mad with fear after such a dream. Regaining her composure, she noted that the window was closed, and everything was in its place.

Leaving her room, Megan attempted to recall where her grandfather's office was located. She stopped in front of one of the doors, feeling that Gregor had pointed her here. Upon entering, she realized it was Malcolm's bedroom. Her heart clenched with sorrow. She caressed the pillow on the bed.

Looking around, Megan noticed another door. The manager had mentioned that the office was next to the bedroom.

Indeed, a few seconds later, she saw Grandpa's desk at the center of the room. To the left there was a lancet window and a bookcase filled with various folders. Behind the chair, on the wall, hung a large canvas in a frame, at the top of which boasted the family coat of arms, and beneath it, the genealogical tree of the McKenzie clan. Sitting at the desk, Megan began to examine the contents of its drawers. In one, she found a bunch of keys mentioned by Warren yesterday. In others, were various documents, seals, and writing instruments. She opened the folder she had brought with her, and for the next two hours, she meticulously studied the affairs of the distillery and all matters related to the upkeep of the castle.

Suddenly, a slight movement at the window caught her attention. Megan froze. Then she turned her head and saw a black raven.

"Oh no! You again! What do you want from me?" she exclaimed with anger and fear. She didn't like this bird at all. "How much more will you harrass me? Can birds even stalk people?! It's just surreal!"

She grabbed the folder and dashed into the corridor. Glenn was heading towards her, "Megan, hi. I thought you'd gone somewhere. I knocked on your bedroom door, but there was no answer. I thought maybe you'd gone with Warren to the distillery. Why do you look so scared? What's happened?"

"Glenn, this might sound silly, but there is a bird that's driving me crazy — a black raven. I've been seeing it every day since I arrived. It's either by the window where I am, or near me in the field, by the shore…everywhere. It scares me! Aren't there any legends related to black ravens here?" The girl desperately fought the urge to break into hysteria.

"It's the first I've ever heard of a raven. Take it easy, Megan. I presume, because of the stress you've recently experienced and the legends you've heard, your nerves are on edge. It's just a bird, don't pay any attention to it."

Seeing as she hadn't convinced Megan, Glenn continued, "Get it out of your head, you're giving too much importance to a trivial matter. You're seeing things that aren't really there. Let's focus on something important, which is why I was looking for you. Since all the representatives of the McKenzie clan are gathering in one place today, there's going to be a kind of celebration. I wanted to suggest you wear a kilt in our colors, if you don't mind. I can show you how to wear it."

"But I don't have a kilt."

"I'll lend you one of mine. We're about the same size."

"I'd be very grateful, and I'd love to wear it — my first time ever," Megan said, calming down and smiling.

"Wonderful! Let's go. Here is mine and Warren's bedroom." Glenn took out everything necessary for Megan's new look from the wardrobe.

"Thank you so much! You're so kind and attentive!"

"No worries, I'm always happy to help you. You can count on me anytime."

"Are you also from here? From the north?" Megan inquired.

"Yes, I'm from Thurso."

"When Warren mentioned that you went to Inverness, I thought you lived there before."

"No. My sister lives in Inverness; her husband is originally from there. When I moved to Castle Mal, my sister stayed with our mother in Thurso, but then she got married two years ago and left our ancestral home. Our father has been gone for a long time, and it's very sad for my mother to be alone. I'm glad she's close. We see each other often. That evening, when you arrived, we were all visiting my sister. She lost her baby in the fourth month of pregnancy, and she's having a very hard time right now."

"I'm so sorry, it's indeed a tragedy."

"Such is life."

"Do you and Warren have children?"

"Not yet, but we haven't lost hope," Glenn said sadly.

"Of course. I'm sure that with time everything will work out and you'll get pregnant. It just isn't your time yet. I know many couples who didn't have children for the first seven or ten years of marriage, and then they had one after another."

"Doctors say everything is fine with us and there's no reason to worry. You know, Megan," the young woman whispered, "last year I asked old lady Innes what she sees. And she predicted that in two years, I would become the mother of a lovely girl. And I believe her! But please, don't tell Warren; I don't want him to know I went to a seer."

"She gave you wonderful news! So, it will happen just like that. How long has it been since your meeting?"

"Eleven months."

"So, you have to wait just a little longer, about four months until you're pregnant," Megan said with a smile.

Glenn's eyes lit up with happiness and anticipation of this joyous moment.

"Megan, what about your personal life? Sorry if the question is inappropriate, you don't have to answer. I won't be offended."

"It's all right, I can easily talk about this topic. I had a boyfriend in London. We dated for more than five years but broke up last year. We realized that the feelings were gone and that we should be free from one another and move on to other things in our lives — real things, you know? I had no time for a relationship. I was always busy with work and my studies. It's amazing how he managed to put up with me for as long as he did. Five years is really overstating it. During that time, we seldom saw each other."

"Wasn't that real love?"

"We had a lot of warmth, respect, and affection for each other. Initially, of course, there was some spark, if you can call it that, but I don't think it was love. I don't know what real love between a man and a woman is. Probably because I've never experienced it. My relationship with Thomas gradually turned into friendship, and nothing more," Megan spoke without emotion.

"Everything has its time, and soon you'll find your happiness."

"I have no doubt about it," the girl laughed.

"Maybe you'll meet someone at the festival! All the men from this area will be there. Choose anyone you want! Warren and I will introduce you to our friends and acquaintances," Glenn said enthusiastically, already mentally picking out a groom for her friend.

"Excellent!" said Megan, hoping for a chance to meet the handsome, mysterious stranger.

8
Castle Raven

"Megan, would you prefer to go by foot or by car?" asked Warren.

"I would love to take a walk."

"Alright, it's not far from here."

Dressed in traditional attire, Warren, his wife, and Megan left the house. Castle Raven was clearly visible from everywhere. It towered over the entire area, unlike Castle Mal, which was situated in a valley by the river. For about fifteen minutes, the owners of both estates climbed the hill. The evening was warm and pleasant. The sea was calm, and the wind occasionally brushed against their faces. A few minutes later, the group arrived at the entrance of the historical castle.

"It's breathtaking!" Megan exclaimed in admiration, trying to take in all the details of the facade. Her gaze fell upon a majestic three-story stone building made of heavy square blocks. On either side, there were four high rectangular towers adorned with battlements, slightly taller than the main building. Above the massive entrance door was a coat of arms unfamiliar to the girl. And from where the castle stood, there was a magnificent view of a series of cliffs stretching into the sea. The area around this historical structure was empty except for the small chapel containing the Drummond family crypt.

"Warren, why is there a bird on the coat of arms?" Megan asked a bit tensely.

"It's a raven, the heraldic symbol of the clan," her cousin responded. "As I told you, the last of the Drummonds disappeared, and Castle Raven passed to the McKenzies. Everything here has been left as it was, in respect of the centuries-old friendship between the clans."

"This bird is now going to haunt me everywhere! And has probably already become my life companion," the girl murmured.

Once in the main hall, she immediately noted a significant difference between this and the hall of the ancestral home. This one seemed a bit gloomier and colder, with heavy bare stone walls. The furniture, made of mahogany, was upholstered in dark burgundy velvet. A huge, antique chandelier hung in the center of the ceiling. A large fireplace was built into the wall, above which was also the family crest of the former owners. Six tall, floor-to-ceiling windows, lined the façade wall. They were decorated with velvet curtains in the same hue as the upholstery, tied back with gold twisted cords and tassels. Like the neighboring castle, this one also housed many hunting trophies.

"This home isn't as modernized as Castle Mal," said Warren.

"Well, that's not modern either," Glenn objected, "but Castle Raven only looks old-fashioned on the ground floor. The last of the Drummonds redesigned the rooms in the style of the late nineteenth century. They're beautiful, cozy and comfortable."

At that moment, Alaric and Duncan came into the hall.

"Oh, I see you've already become a true McKenzie," Duncan said, carefully examining his cousin's outfit.

"Our colors suit you very well," Alaric said approvingly.

"Thank you, I'm glad to see you both."

In reality, Megan felt quite awkward in their presence. She very much wished for the lingering tension, left after the family meeting, to finally dissipate so they could interact without strain.

"Really?" Duncan asked with a hint of sarcasm.

Warren intervened before anyone could comment further, "How's it going, bro?" Getting ready for Witch's Night?" he cheerfully said, clapping his brother on the shoulder as a greeting. "We've already introduced our relative to the local traditions and recounted the legends of this region. She's eagerly awaiting the festival!"

Megan inwardly thanked Warren for finding a way out of the awkward situation Duncan had created with his question. It seemed the younger of her cousins was not yet ready to let go of the suspicion she had cast on their family.

"That's wonderful! It's high time she joined our traditions and celebrations," Alaric said amiably.

"How are you doing, Megan? Have you settled in? How were your days at Castle Mal?"

"Very eventful! We visited the distillery yesterday, and I got acquainted with the production technology. It was interesting to learn and see all this with my own eyes."

"I'm happy for you, girl! Duncan, go show our guest around the castle!" the eldest of the clan told his grandson.

"With pleasure! Megan, would you mind if I act as your guide for the next half-hour?" he asked with a wry smile.

"I'll be grateful for that!" the girl responded as friendly as possible.

They walked through a stone arch that divided the hall, leading to a wide semicircular staircase with beautiful stone railings. In the flight between the floors, there was a lancet window framed by carved wooden molding. On the windowsill, designed as a bench, lay two decorative pillows made of dark red velvet. The upper floor extended into a gallery, from which there was a view of the hall situated below. Portraits of the Drummond clan members hung on the walls of the gallery. Megan admired everything around her. When they reached the residential area, Duncan opened one of the doors, saying, "Guest room. If you decide to stay in Castle Raven, you're more than welcome. We would be glad."

The girl liked what she saw. Walls draped in blue silk; a bedspread on the large double bed with the same hue, standing opposite the entrance; a canopy with golden edging, and high windows on either side of the bed. It was a complete surprise to see such a cozy, warm chamber after the somewhat gloomy nature of the lower floor.

"Practically all the rooms have been modified and improved. The last representative of the clan wanted them all to match the era's style. This bedroom was intended for the future mistress of the castle," the cousin explained.

"For Margaret?! Warren told me this tragic tale yesterday," Megan exclaimed with passion mixed with surprise.

"Yes, for her. And this inner door," Duncan swung it open for his companion, "leads to the lord's bedchamber. Voilà!" he sang cheerfully.

The girl eagerly entered. The room was slightly larger than the neighboring one. Dark blue tones, gold trim, more heavy grand furniture, a serious style – everything indicated that a man lived here. Above the headboard of the bed hung the clan's coat of arms.

"Does anyone live here?"

"Nope. Our ancestors didn't touch it for a long time, hoping that Drummond would return. Time passed, generations changed, but it remained uninhabited. There are many other comfortable bedrooms in the house, so let this one remain for the spirit of the lost lord," Duncan said theatrically, with an angelic smile, amusing Megan greatly.

"Are there really ghosts in here?" she asked skeptically.

"Are you afraid of them? Then come stay with us! Let's see if the spirit of Drummond comes to meet you if you take his former fiancée's apartment. Then you can tell us what he reveals to you," Duncan joked, thoroughly enjoying the opportunity to tease Megan.

"Not funny! Now I definitely won't stay with you. You can ask him everything you want to know yourself, and then tell me," she retorted cheerfully.

"What a coward! I'm joking, of course, there are no spirits here and there never have been. Otherwise, we would have met them long ago. Let's move on, otherwise, while you're looking around here, I'll miss dinner. And that I definitely won't forgive!" the young man smiled.

They went to one of the castle towers and found themselves in a large library. Megan was surrounded by tall shelves filled with a rich collection of books.

"What beauty! I love books so much! I could spend days here without leaving," she said dreamily. The girl ran her hand over the spines, enjoying the opportunity to touch history. The library housed editions dating back to the 18th century and later. Her gaze quickly scanned the long row of unusual bindings and settled on the legends and tales of Scotland. I mustn't lose sight of these, she thought. I'd like to look at these first.

"What's there?" she pointed to a small door built into one of the bookshelves. It was clear that it led somewhere.

"Something like a storeroom. Paintings, portraits, personal belongings of the Drummonds. No one has cleaned it for about a hundred years. Once, as a child, I wanted to hide there but I got caught in a web, and a spider fell on my face. I ran out of there screaming and never again felt the urge to enter that dreadful place."

"A spider isn't as scary as a ghost."

"To each their own! I've never encountered ghosts. But spiders are absolutely real and very unpleasant creatures," Duncan said with slight disgust.

In a good mood, with playful comments, Duncan showed Megan several more rooms, and then they went into the dining hall where they were expected.

During dinner, they discussed many different topics, and the girl's relatives took a keen interest in her London life. Everyone there seemed to have decided not to bring up the unpleasant conversation from the day of the meeting. They all acted as if nothing had happened, although Megan was sure that such things are hard to forget.

"Megan, allow me to ask you a provocative question!" exclaimed Alaric, smiling warmly, "Have you started to miss London yet?"

"Indeed, a provocative question!" Megan smiled in response. "In the last few days, I've been discovering a new world. Breathtaking castles! Incredible heather fields! The mystique and history of my family – all of it truly fascinates and attracts me. I don't remember London making such an impression on me. But I'll admit, I do miss its noise and the fast pace of life."

"I see," the elderly man said thoughtfully, cutting a piece of venison.

Dinner went smoothly and comfortably, and afterward, everyone gathered in the hall by the fireplace.

"Having a glass of good whiskey after dinner is one of our family traditions," Alaric said with a satisfied smile.

"Warren introduced me to this tradition at Castle Mal yesterday," Megan responded. "He and Glenn told me a lot of interesting things. Though, I'm very impressionable, and it led me to have nightmares all night."

"I warned you, since you take everything to heart, you'd be scared at night! But your curiosity overcame your fear," Warren joined in.

"Yes, that's true. I dreamt about Margaret and Mary, the crypt, my grandfather..."

"Well, now that I showed you Margaret's and the lost lord's rooms, you won't sleep tonight either!" Duncan said, laughing merrily.

"No, it's all good. I truly found it very fascinating. They had such a sad story," Megan said thoughtfully.

"That's life. It's not the first nor the last sad love story in the world," concluded Alaric.

The McKenzie family spent another hour and a half by the fireplace. Megan, holding a glass of whiskey, watched the dancing flames and felt the warmth spread through her body.

"It's getting late, we should head back," Warren said, placing his empty glass on the coffee table.

After thanking her relatives for such a magical evening, Megan slowly headed for the exit. Seeing her off, Alaric said, "Our doors are always open to you, girl. I'm very glad you came. Do visit us more often. We'll be very happy to see you!"

"Thank you for your hospitality and kind words, I appreciate it!" she responded with a warm smile.

In the moonless night, Megan could hardly make out the silhouettes of her companions. She liked this couple; the spouses were harmonious, kind, and sensible. With them, she felt comfortable and confident. Warren was open-hearted and sweet, never prone to sudden mood swings, and Glenn was gentle, empathetic, and always ready to help — they were comfortable in life and saw positivity and joy in everything.

Wishing them a good night, Megan hurried to her room. Eagerly, she rushed to the window, flung it open, but there was nobody outside. She very much wanted to go to the hill, to wait for him there, but the fear associated with the risk of another attempt on her life held her back. She looked at the mantle clock – 10:10 p.m. He will definitely come, I just need to wait a bit longer, she thought.

The girl picked up the folder, flipped through the papers, but couldn't concentrate. Setting the documents aside, she started pacing back and forth in her room, like a tiger in a cage, once again confirming that there's nothing worse than waiting. She checked the clock again and was surprised to see it was only 10:35 p.m. It felt like weeks had passed. Once more, she approached the window, and her heart raced at the sight of a man's silhouette in a kilt. All her rational thoughts switched off instantly. Rushing out of her room, Megan flew down the stairs. Fortunately, she didn't encounter anyone in the hall. But a faint voice of reason, cutting through the thick fog of emotions, tried to caution her. She decided to take a knife from the kitchen so that she could defend herself if necessary. Tucking her acquisition behind the belt of her kilt and covering it with her cape, she left the castle. Looking around, she silently made her way to where she had seen the mysterious stranger.

He was standing with his back to her, looking towards the sea. The light from Megan's window illuminated his tall, beautiful, well-built, and sturdy figure. The Scottish outfit fit him impeccably. High black hose socks, a black kilt with a dark gray check pattern, a black jacket, over which a tartan cloth matching the kilt was thrown over the left shoulder. A black beret on his head blended with his black hair. To Megan, the man seemed mysterious, yet perfect. Walking quietly on the grass, she approached him, trying to get closer, unnoticingly. Her hands and legs were trembling. Overwhelmed with excitement and anticipation, only now did she start to realize that she was afraid, but she could no longer turn back. It was vitally important for her to find out who he was. An incredible force of attraction pulled her entire being towards this man. His appearance was mesmerizing. Just as she was about to touch the highlander's shoulder, he calmly turned towards her, as if he had always known she was there, just waiting for her to come closer. Megan covered her mouth with her hand in a silent scream. Her eyes widened with fear, but she couldn't look away from the stranger. He looked at her impassively and silently. Megan realized he was not going to start the conversation, and, summoning the last of her courage, she asked, "Who are you?"

There was a brief silence. He continued to look into her eyes without blinking.

"Derek. My name is Derek." His face remained calm and serene.

She couldn't read any emotions on it, "Why do you come here in the evenings?"

He calmly replied, "I found out someone tried to kill you. By chance, I was here then. Now, I make sure that this person doesn't come back again."

"But it wasn't you who saved me then. The man who attacked me was stopped by a bird."

"After you lost consciousness, I carried you to your bedroom."

"I figured it was you. But how did you know which room was mine?" Megan asked with some insistence. By this point, she had regained her composure, thus managing to control her trembling.

"I saw your reflection in the window before you left the castle. It's not hard to guess where your bedroom is based on the window," Derek replied, still calmly and undisturbed.

"Where are you from?"

"I'm local, we're neighbors, you could say."

"My name is Megan," she introduced herself, slightly satisfied with his answers.

A faint smile touched Derek's lips — the first emotion since the start of their conversation. From the expression on the highlander's handsome face, it was clear he already knew the girl's name.

"Nice to meet you, Megan. Glad to make your acquaintance. Why are you outside at such a late hour? It's dangerous. The attack could be repeated, and I might not be nearby to protect you."

"I saw you and decided to find out who you are, and what your intentions are by coming here."

"Are you satisfied with your curiosity?" he asked, still with that slight smile.

"Not entirely. Why do you need to do this?"

"Do what exactly?"

"Protect me, for example. You say you come here to see if the murderer shows up again. Why do you need to do this?" Megan asked, shifting back to a more emotional tone.

He was silent for a moment before answering.

"You will find out in time. Now go home and go to sleep. That man is not nearby."

"Do you know him? Who is he? And why does he want to kill me?" Megan asked anxiously.

"I don't know yet, but the time will come when everything will be clear."

"I..."

But Derek did not let her continue. The tone in his voice changed, he said sternly and authoritatively, "Go to sleep, Megan!"

She did not dare to object. The command was so categorical and unexpected that she could not find the words to respond. At that moment, the cold and harsh expression on the man's face made it clear that he was not intending to continue their conversation. Megan silently turned around and walked back to the castle. Inside, she was seething with indignation: he had given her an order! And she had been too flustered to put him in his place.

Derek watched her until she disappeared from view. With a sigh of sadness, he turned back to the sea. He knew the girl would watch him from her bedroom window for a few more minutes, but he did not turn around.

*****

Megan couldn't sleep. The Highlander's inexplicable behavior greatly troubled her. He was so strange, mysterious. One thing she knew for sure — she needed to talk to him again; learn more about him. And at the very least make it clear that it's not alright for anyone to speak to her in a commanding tone. The beautiful, inscrutable face constantly hovered before her eyes. She had never before felt such a passionate desire to kiss a man. A French kiss — yes, but to want to kiss, besides the lips, his cheeks, nose, eyes, forehead. This was new to her. She desperately wanted to press herself against his chest and drown in his embrace.

Megan finally stopped understanding what was happening to her. Knowing nothing about the man except his name, to experience such mixed feelings: anger and ecstasy, curiosity and passion. It made her doubt her sanity.

When the girl finally dozed off, the dream where a man whispered her name, standing by her bed, and then kissing her, unexpectedly resurfaced in her memory. And in the morning, she found the window in her room open. It was him, Derek! That's why his face seemed so familiar. Realizing all this, Megan sat up abruptly.

"So, who are you?" she whispered, puzzled.

9
The Fern Festival

The inhabitants of Castle Mal and Castle Raven were preparing for the festival. For three days, Megan could not find peace. Every evening, from ten o'clock to three in the morning, she looked out the window every fifteen minutes, searching for Derek, but he never appeared. She asked Glenn and Warren about a neighbor named Derek, but they responded negatively — there were no neighbors by that name in their vicinity. During these three days, she covered many miles on foot, exploring the surroundings of both castles in hopes of encountering him somewhere. Now she could only hope for his presence at the festival, where she could ask him the questions that had been tormenting her lately.

Finally, the day of the fern festival arrived. Malcolm McKenzie's granddaughter, dressed in a kilt and cape, carefully examined every detail of her appearance in the mirror when Glenn knocked on the door.

"Megan, are you ready? Warren is waiting for us downstairs."

"Yes, we can go. Glenn, did I fasten everything correctly?"

"Everything is fine, you look magnificent. If only your grandfather could see you now! Let's go, it's time!"

The celebrations took place very close by. All over the field, there were preparations for bonfires. Bonfires had a dual significance in folk customs. They were associated with the sun and believed to have purifying properties. According to ancient beliefs, the flame protected a person from evil, witchcraft, and impure forces. It was precisely on this night that the boundaries between the world of humans and the supernatural realms blurred, allowing evil spirits to guard the magical fern flower.

Numerous tents stretched along the field, offering a variety of foods, while beer, ale, and whisky were sold in every third stall, attracting the longest queues. The aroma of hot stewed lamb and venison wafted from some tents and different types of sausages and frankfurters were grilled on coals right on the spot. Children's eyes widened at the sight of various sweets, cotton candy, and balloons. Opposite the tents, rows of wooden tables with benches were set up. Bagpipers played around other musicians and dancers in national costumes performed captivating folk dances. Voices buzzed and laughter rang out from all directions. The crowd mostly moved around the field; only a few sat at tables, everyone was eager to socialize. People walked towards each other, encountering familiar faces at every step, stopping to exchange a few words. Several tourists mingled with the locals, drinking ale and taking photos of everything that seemed interesting and engaging.

"It's such a nice atmosphere," Megan remarked.

"I like it too! Warren, look, there's Alaric! Let's go say hello," Glenn suggested.

The head of the McKenzie clan stood with a pint of ale among a group of adult males, engaging in a lively and cheerful discussion.

"Ah, here come the youngsters!" Alaric joyfully said, giving Warren a friendly slap on the shoulder.

"Friends, let me introduce you to Megan, Malcolm's granddaughter. She arrived here a few days ago."

Megan greeted them. The new acquaintances were curious indeed; they asked her about life in London and her impressions of Scotland. She responded, but eagerly awaited the chance to leave the adult company. After twenty minutes, she took advantage of a brief pause to ask Alaric, "Have you seen Duncan? Is he at the festival?"

"Yes, we came together, but he opted for some younger companions; he's here somewhere. I suggest you look for a group of young ladies, Duncan will surely be at the center," he laughed.

"Oh, that Duncan!" chuckled one of the older men. Everyone began to jovially discuss Duncan's love- persuits.

"I'll go look for him. Thank you for the advice," Megan smiled.

In a moment, she blended into the crowd, trying to quickly disappear from the elders' view, before they have a chance to stop her. In reality, she wasn't really looking for her cousin but needed an excuse. She aimlessly wandered past the tents, peering into the faces of passersby, in hopes of seeing Derek. Roaming the fair, she didn't notice how quickly time flew by. The sun had set, and she had neither encountered Derek nor any of her relatives. Some drunk men tried to strike up conversations with her, as the festival was in full swing. People grouped together around tables overloaded with food and drinks. Ritual fires were lit all around the fairground, illuminating the surroundings with their bright light.

Megan felt tired after several hours of walking. She was looking for a place to sit, but now all the seats were taken. Ordering a pint of ale at one of the tents, she asked what time it was.

"It's only 10:15. The fern hasn't bloomed yet," said the man with a smile, handing her the drink.

Moving among the celebrators, it was possible to catch snippets of conversation. Many spoke of the mystical plant. Some sincerely believed in its blooming, others mocked the believers, especially those who planned to search for it at midnight. However, Megan didn't pay much attention, as she was occupied with searching for Derek and had no intention of wandering the dark forest at night, in the hope of finding a mythical flower, which may or may not exist. Her gaze quickly scanned the faces around the tables.

As she moved away from the crowd, the hum of voices grew faintor. She walked down towards the river. Behind her, the folk festivities and the reflections of burning fires remained. She sat on one of the large stones at the water's edge and thoughtfully looked ahead. There, on the hill, stood

Castle Raven, and to the left, in the valley, was Castle Mal. They created such a beautiful and harmonious picture.

Megan turned abruptly when she felt someone sit beside her. And there he was, the one she had been waiting for. Calmly and silently, he gazed at the river.

"Derek!" I've been looking for you." Her heart began pounding with joy.

"Really?" he asked, shifting his gaze from the river to her.

"You were in my room, not only the night I was attacked, but the other night too. You kissed me. I realized it wasn't a dream. Why did you secretly sneak into the castle in the middle of the night? You say you're protecting me, but you appear in my bedroom and ignore my questions. Who the hell are you? And what do you want from me?" Megan asked assertively, eager for answers.

"So many questions, Miss McKenzie. Where shall I start?" he asked with a slight smile on his face.

"Why did you come to my room?"

"To bring you back after you fainted," Derek stubbornly pretended as if he hadn't understood which night she was referring to.

"You know perfectly well I'm talking about your other visit. You were in my bedroom, whispering my name, kissing me!"

"Ah, that night… You enchanted me with your beauty. I couldn't resist; I had a strong desire to kiss you."

"So, you really believe this barbaric tactic, of sneaking into the castle while I'm asleep, kissing me, and then jumping out of the window from the second floor, is a good approach?

The Magic Ring of Brodgar | 75

Lucky you didn't break your neck," she smirked for the first time, seeing his broad and genuine smile.

"I thought it was rather romantic, not barbaric," he teased her.

Megan was astonished by the unfolding of events, while he found it genuinely amusing. On one hand, she was angry that he ignored her questions or made light of them. Yet, at the same time, she felt joy that he was here. He had found her.

"Tell me, who are you?"

"I'm Derek."

"You've already told me that. Where do you live?"

"Not far from here."

"No one here knows anyone by the name of Derek."

He continued to speak with a smile, never taking his eyes off her. "Really? You've already inquired? You've taken quite an interest in me; I'm flattered."

"Yes, quite an interest. Because you're a strange individual."

"It only seems that way to you. I'm just an ordinary person, absolutely normal."

"It's odd, to say the least, that you stand on the hill outside the castle every night."

"Not every night."

"Fine, not every night. But you're watching me!"

"I see nothing strange in this." Derek kept bouncing the questions back at her, smiling playfully.

After a short pause, he added, "I'm from Thurso, that's why you couldn't find any information about me."

"I see," muttered Megan, feeling foolish. Mentally she tried to analyze the situation: perhaps there really was nothing strange. She might have imagined all these absurdities and believed in them. Perhaps Derek just stood near the castle on the first evening, enjoying the scenery, and after seeing that she was in danger, carried her safely to her room. Maybe she appealed to him, and decided to get acquainted with her in this unusual way. Methods of acquaintance do vary. Derek, presumably, preferred this one. After all, they are Highlanders; perhaps this is their custom.

"Are you going after the fern flower?" Derek asked with a grin.

"No, of course not."

"Why so categorically?"

"Firstly, I don't believe in it. Secondly, I'm afraid of the dark and anything unexplainable."

"Really?" he asked, smiling enigmatically.

"Yes really. And do you believe in these fairy tales?"

"The fern blooming once a year is an absolute fact. And I am not afraid of the darkness or the inexplicable," he answered with a serious expression on his face.

"I hope you're not saying that you've once picked the flower and now possess magical powers?" she teased him.

"I have never picked a fern flower, and I do not have any magical powers," Derek said just as seriously.

"That's good to know, because I was starting to get scared."

"Scared of what?"

"Well, as I've already mentioned, I'm afraid of what can't be explained."

"But even the inexplicable can be explained; don't you agree?"

"I don't know. But I do know that I don't like this topic," Megan responded, frowning.

"Did you enjoy the festival?"

"Yes, I did."

"How long are you planning to stay here, Megan?"

"Another week, I think, and then it'll be time to go back home," she answered with a slight sadness in her voice.

At these words, he grew more serious and thoughtful.

"And who will manage the distillery?"

"I suppose my cousin Warren will. Wait, how do you know about the distillery?" Megan asked surprised.

"Everyone around here knows about it," Derek smiled and again lapsed into silence.

After waiting a bit, the girl asked, "What are you thinking about so deeply?"

"You," he said with a smile.

"And more specifically?"

"If you leave, how will I live without you?" He seemed to be joking, but her heart beat faster at these words.

Suddenly Derek pulled her close and kissed her passionately. Megan's head spun and her chest pounded so loudly that she thought even he could hear it. She was overwhelmed by a whirlwind of emotions. This kiss was the sweetest she's had in her life.

Derek looked into her eyes.

Megan thought about the astonishing feeling taking over her, as if she has known Derek for a long time. He felt so familiar and beloved to her. Her entire being was drawn to him. Her soul sought his. The girl ran her finger across his face, from his temple to his chin, carefully studying his handsome features. Flawless skin, precise eyebrows, dark thick hair. Today, Megan noticed, he wasn't wearing his beret.

"You're admiring me?" he asked with a smile.

"Yes, you're remarkably attractive; how old are you?"

He was silent for a moment, continuing to gaze at her intently.

"I'm twenty-nine," he said after the brief pause.

"What do you do for a living? Where do you work?"

He did not seem to expect this question and wasn't ready to answer it right away. It was the first time Megan saw him at a loss.

"I work in the city administration of Thurso," he said calmly after a moment's hesitation.

"And what about you? What do you do in London?"

"How did you know I'm from London?"

"You're originally from here, you just live in London," he emphasized. "Everyone knows the story about how your mother left this place many years ago, being pregnant with you."

"Yes, that's right. I keep forgetting that this is a village. Everyone knows everything about each other. I own a restaurant; my mom opened it many years ago. She moved to America to live with her husband while I stayed in London. Sam, the restaurant manager, helps me out. He's great; without him, I wouldn't have been able to do it."

"You're great, Megan."

"Thanks. Have you got family? Brothers, sisters?"

"I was an only child. My father and mother have long passed away."

"I'm sorry to hear that."

"I'm used to being alone," he said calmly and emotionlessly.

"You know, me too," she said, smiling. "Do you hear that? The sounds of bagpipes have nearly fallen silent. Everyone has probably gone looking for the flower."

"Are you scared?"

"No. After all, you're here with me."

"I'm glad you feel safe in my presence."

"I think my family is worried about my disappearance. I left them at the beginning of the festival. They don't know where I am. I need to go. I don't want to cause any panic."

"Responsibility is one of the main traits of your character," he smirked. "Let's go, I'll walk you back."

They walked slowly towards her home, enjoying each other's company. It had completely darkened. The moon was entirely hidden behind the clouds. Without getting too close to the castle, Derek embraced Megan, kissed her goodbye, and wished her a good night. She expected him to suggest meeting again or to set a date, but he remained silent. Apparently, he was the type of man who decided when and where the next meeting would occur before letting others know. Discussions and agreements were not his style.

"Good night, Derek," said the girl, and walked away without looking back.

Closing the door behind her, she stole a quick glance at the spot where they had just said goodbye, but he was no longer there.

"Megan! We were looking for you, where did you go? I was so worried. We couldn't find you among the people at the celebration, so we thought you had returned home before us, but imagine our horror when we didn't find you here either."

"Sorry, Glenn. I met a young man, we got to talking, and I lost track of time."

"Well, that's a pretty good reason," Glenn said approvingly.

"What time is it?"

"Past one in the morning."

"Oh, that's late indeed."

"It's okay, don't worry. I'll go calm Warren down. He went up to our room for his jacket and was about to go out looking for you."

"Megan! Thank God you're back!" her cousin was already descending the staircase.

"I'm sorry; I really didn't mean to worry you."

"Everything's fine. The main thing is you're home and you're safe. Now we can all sleep in peace."

All three went upstairs and dispersed to their rooms. Megan was happy. She remembered Derek; his handsome face, his kisses, and realized that she didn't want to leave for London anymore. A light, dreamy smile appeared on her lips as she went to bed, full of anticipation for their future meetings. That night, the girl slept soundly and sweetly, without any dreams.

*****

In the morning, Megan invited Gregor to Malcolm's office to discuss some points about the documents he had handed over to her a few days ago. The manager meticulously answered Megan's questions and helped her analyze all aspects of the work. Pleased with the results of their brief meeting, she let him go.

Now that I have studied all the information, it's time to make a decision, she thought. There seemed to be only one decision to make — appoint Warren as the head of the factory, leave him in charge of Castle Mal, and head back to London. The castle, in any case, needed to stay in reliable hands. Someone had to live in it to prevent it from falling into disrepair. But Megan had no desire to leave at the moment; after all, Derek had come into her life. She pondered for a long time on what to do. The family meeting was scheduled in three days, and she would have to announce her decision. First of all, it was necessary to talk to Warren, offer him management responsibility with a fifty-fifty profit split. She had no desire to manage the work personally, as the restaurant business required her full commitment.

She could stay a few more weeks at Castle Mal to see how events would unfold. Extending her stay in her historical homeland would not be too bad. The only thing left was to make arrangements with her cousin. Leaving the office, she went down to the hall.

"Glenn, do you know where Warren is?"

"He left for the distillery this morning."

"Did he say what time he'd be back?"

"No, he always returns at different times. If I see him before you do, I'll definitely tell him you were looking for him."

"Thank you."

"I hope you had a successful introduction yesterday. Warren and I wanted to introduce you to our friends. If you're interested, we can arrange, for example, a friendly lunch or dinner in the coming days."

"Why not? Meeting new people is always useful. Yesterday's rendezvous was quite ordinary, nothing special," said Megan, feigning indifference. She didn't like discussing her personal life, so she decided not to mention anything about Derek just yet. There was still nothing between them, and perhaps there never will be.

"Glenn, if you're not busy right now, shall we go for a walk? I'd like to bring some heather back to my room."

"I'd love to join you. Just let me grab my wrap. It's always chilly with the sea breeze."

For the next two hours, Megan and Glenn strolled along the beach and through the heather fields. They got to know each other better, chatting non-stop and discovering their differences. Megan was reserved and usually only talked about what she considered safe. She could carry any conversation, but skillfully changed the subject when necessary, so her interlocutor could hardly notice the shift. She only superficially touched on personal matters. Glenn was much more sociable. Always ready to share her thoughts, experiences, and hopes — she never seemed gossipy or pushy. She had a fine sense of when someone didn't want to talk about something and tactfully changed the subject. She was interested in everything around her and listened to her company with joy and attention. Megan felt easy and calm with Glenn.

When they returned to the castle, Warren was already waiting for them.

"There you are! I was wondering where you had disappeared to."

"Megan wanted to pick some heather, and I decided to keep her company."

"Warren, I was looking for you earlier today. I'd like to discuss some important matters," Megan got straight to the point.

"Sure, whenever it's convenient for you."

"If you're free now, then I'm ready."

"Then let's go to Malcolm's office," the cousin suggested.

It took them about an hour to discuss all the details. Warren was receptive to the idea of staying in the castle and taking over the management of the distillery. He thought it was the best solution to the problem.

"I think I'll stay here a bit longer. A few weeks of vacation will do me good. I've enjoyed the peaceful, measured life here, unlike London, where every day is just hustle and bustle," Megan said.

"Excellent news! Glenn and I would be delighted. The more frequent and longer your visits, the better. Glenn is so happy with your friendship. She missed that. She has become very attached to you."

"Thank you, Warren, I'm also very glad that we became friends. By the way, I think it's time to eat something."

They went downstairs, where Glenn was eagerly waiting for them.

"It's so good you came, I'm so hungry. I thought if you didn't come in ten minutes, I'd start dinner without you," she said, neatly folding the wrapper from a candy she just ate.

"What's with you today? Where does this appetite come from?" Warren asked.

"I burned hundreds of calories today! Your cousin and I walked many miles. I probably broke my weekly record in one day," Glenn laughed.

Dinner was pleasant and cheerful, but Megan couldn't wait to go up to her room and look out the window. She was anxious and thought only, will he come tonight? Every day of her life had become one continuous wait. Every few minutes, she looked at the hill in hopes of seeing him, but in vain — Derek did not appear that evening. Only at dawn did the girl finally fall asleep.

*****

All morning Megan was tormented by theories as to why he hadn't come. Perhaps he decided not to appear in her life at all anymore? She was suffering, not knowing how to pass the time until the evening. Assessing her own state of mind, she found it highly disturbing. The girl justified her restlessness and confusion by the lack of activities here; she was used to the busy schedule and dynamic life of a metropolis. The first half of the day was drowned in idleness.

When Megan came down for lunch, her relatives were already waiting for her.

"Warren, I keep forgetting to ask, what does the tree and sword on the family crest mean?" she inquired.

"The tree is a Celtic symbol of life. The meaning is that the McKenzies are firmly grounded, having set their roots, and the sword is nothing other than a symbol of bravery and valor of the clan's members."

"And why do the Drummonds have a raven on their coat of arms? What does that signify?"

"According to one legend, the founder of the Drummond clan was a tall, thin, dark-haired man. He dressed in black and probably resembled a raven. Members of his family were nicknamed The Ravens by the people. They were all dark-haired. After some time, he decided that this bird would be on his clan's crest. But don't be afraid, Megan. They were not warlocks and had no association with magic. The Drummonds were honorable people, just like the McKenzies, and there was never any conflict between our families."

"Thank you, Warren. I've learned so much these days, it's incredible. By the way, I really wanted to visit the neighboring islands. Can we go on a tour there? I can't wait to see them," Megan asked with genuine interest.

"If you like, we can go there tomorrow."

"That would be great."

The girl sighed with relief, finding a way to spend another day.

"Megan, tonight our family plans to have dinner at one of our favorite restaurants in town. Will you join us?" asked Warren.

"With pleasure."

After lunch, the girl headed to the library she had discovered a few days ago while roaming around the castle, and continued to explore the vast rows of ancient books. Reading was one of her most favorite hobbies. Moreover, just as in Castle Raven, she found a book of Scottish tales and legends on a shelf and reached for the thick, old, ancient volume with remnants of a greenish image on the cover.

She binge-read stories about the mysteries of Scottish castles, about the blood shed within them, and the bodiless spirits forever locked within these stone walls. Here, she also learned that many Scottish families had their own spirits or house ghosts. She became so engrossed in the history and her own thoughts about it that she didn't notice how quickly the time had passed.

10
What Is Love?

The restaurant chosen for dinner specialized in game dishes, and its interior was largely adorned with hunting trophies.

"This is the best place in town. Malcolm and I used to come here often for freshly brewed ale and delicious meat," Alaric recalled, smiling as he remembered the good old times.

"You won't find better game preparation anywhere else," Duncan added.

"You praise the local cuisine so much that I can't wait to try everything," Megan laughed.

Ordering various dishes of wild boar, venison, duck, hare, they drank ale and enjoyed the food. The conversation throughout the evening revolved around the factories; they also discussed the latest local news. Megan didn't wait for the planned family meeting to announce her decision and share her plans, which she had previously discussed with Warren.

Alaric was pleased with this turn of events, saying, "I think you made the right decision. It's quite hard to split your time between two cities and manage two enterprises. Warren is a worthy candidate and will handle the business well. You are a member of our family. This is your home, and you are welcome here anytime. We will always be happy to see you."

"I completely agree," Duncan chimed in approvingly.

At that moment, a man in his thirties approached their table: tall, broad-shouldered, with light hair and green eyes. The McKenzie men warmly greeted him – he turned out to be an old friend of Warren's. Without much thought, Alaric invited him to join them at the table.

"Craig, I'd like to introduce you to my cousin Megan. She's Malcolm's granddaughter. She came to take care of her inheritance and decide its fate," Warren explained.

"Nice to meet you," Craig said, looking at her with an admiring smile, extending his strong firm arm for a handshake.

Megan found the highlander quite attractive. It seemed that the feeling was mutual because throughout the evening, almost all his attention was directed at her. Craig clearly wanted to learn as much about the girl as possible, and she happily engaged in conversation, enjoying the company of the young man and her family members.

"Craig, what do you do for a living?" she inquired.

"I work for one of the local shipping companies."

"Tomorrow we're using one of your ferries to get to the island," Warren said.

"Really? What are you heading there for?"

"We're going to sacrifice Megan on the altar of the druids," joked the younger cousin.

"Thanks, Duncan. At least I know the real purpose of our journey now," Megan laughed.

"If you don't mind, I'd like to come along," the young man said, looking hopefully at the girl.

"Of course, you're welcome to join us. Megan, you don't mind, do you?" Duncan asked.

"Of course not."

"What time will you be at the dock tomorrow morning?" he asked Warren.

"I think we'll arrive by eleven thirty."

"Well, Megan, prepare yourself! You're in for an unforgettable experience, since it will be conducted by true local highlanders," Craig said with a proud smile.

"I'm looking forward to it," she replied cheerfully.

After dinner, everyone said their goodbyes, and went their separate ways. On the drive home, Warren said, "Megan, in just one evening, you've charmed my friend. I've known him for a long time, and he's already smitten with you."

"Is he always so quick to fall in love?" she laughed.

"No, quite the opposite! I can't remember the last time he was so enchanted by a woman. Since Craig decided to join us tomorrow, it means he wants to get to know you better."

"Did you like him? He's quite interesting and handsome, isn't he?" Glenn chattered.

"Glenn!" Warren protested.

"What did I say? I just asked if she liked him. I would be really happy if she found her love here and stayed with us."

"I understand you'd be happy, but it's tactless to ask such questions. They've known each other for a few hours, and you're probably already imagining a wedding and a bunch of kids in your romantic fantasies. Let people get to know each other better and then we'll see."

"Don't worry, Warren. We're women and it's normal for us to ask such questions. Craig is certainly a charismatic and handsome young man, in my opinion. But it's too soon to say anything more. We barely know each other to draw any conclusions."

As they arrived at the castle, Megan checked the time; it was already 11:10. Her heart beat faster. Was he waiting for her tonight? What if he came, saw no light in her window, and left?

She eagerly anticipated their next meeting and feared it might not happen anytime soon.

After wishing Warren and Glenn goodnight, Megan rushed to her room and ran to the window. He was there, on the hill, waiting for her. Her hands trembled, butterflies fluttered in her stomach, and a joyful smile lit up her face. Without a second thought, she quickly left the castle.

Coming close to Derek, she said, "I'm glad you came; I was waiting for you."

He smiled, brushed a stray lock of hair from her face, and kissed her.

"I'm glad to see you too," he whispered softly in her ear.

"Derek, I don't understand why all the mystery? These meetings under my window, without any warning… It's as if we're living in the Middle Ages and there's no other way to meet. Can't we do it differently?"

"You don't like this?" he asked with a barely noticeable smile.

"Well, it's a bit strange."

"I work late every day."

"Don't you have any days off?" Megan asked surprised.

"Not at the moment. I'm currently working on a secret project, and I'm only free in the evenings."

"There are secret projects in city administration? I never thought that was a thing," she said dubiously.

"I can't explain everything to you yet. It's not just about the city administration. I've signed nondisclosure agreements regarding my current mission. So, please don't ask me about my work for now. I'll definitely tell you everything when the time comes. This... mystery, as you call it, is temporary."

"Alright, I understand. Non-disclosure means nondisclosure. You're probably a 007 agent," she joked.

Derek just smiled, "How was your evening?" he said, changing the subject.

"Very good, I wasn't as bored today as I was on the other days."

"Who entertained you?" he inquired.

In his question, Megan sensed strange notes, as if he knew about her new acquaintance.

"We had a family dinner," she shared without going into details.

"I'm glad you had a good time. Would you mind taking a walk with me? We could go down to the sea or up the hill."

"I'd love to," she responded, happy for the opportunity to spend more time together.

Derek wrapped his arm around her waist, and they headed towards the beach. Megan was dressed warmly, so the light breeze blowing from the sea didn't bother her. Large boulders were scattered across the sand. The young man sat down on one of them and pulled her close. They sat there for a long time, talking about various topics. The conversation flowed easily and naturally. Megan noted to herself that Derek was intelligent, well-educated, and knowledgeable on many issues; with his wisdom and tact she felt they could discuss anything and everything. He seemed perfect. For the first time in her life, she felt truly happy, spending almost the entire night in his strong embrace.

"You know, Derek, I find myself liking you more and more," she said with a smile, gazing into his eyes.

"Thank you, I'm flattered. And what did I do to earn such affection today?" he asked, cocking his right eyebrow.

"You're smart…, interesting. It's very easy and comfortable to talk to you."

"The feeling is mutual."

"It's hard to believe that one person can embody incredible beauty, wisdom, romanticism, and so much more," she continued.

"So many compliments! You're idealizing me, I'm embarrassed," he laughed.

"I'm not idealizing. Actually, I was thinking… there must be at least one flaw in you! Tell me, what's not right, what am I not seeing?" she playfully said.

"Like everyone, I have my downsides."

"Such as?"

"The most serious one you'll find out about later," Derek said, devoid of any emotion.

"You're a sadist? Or a maniac?"

His loud laughter broke the silence of the night. It was the first time Megan had heard Derek laugh so genuinely and contagiously. The suggestion amused him greatly.

"Why of all things did you come up with these ones?" he asked, still laughing.

"I don't know," Megan chuckled.

"Your guesses are wrong. Any other ideas?"

"You're not really a 007 agent, are you?" she asked, making a disapproving face.

"What an imagination you have!"

"I can't think of anything else. You tell me," Megan insisted.

"In time, you'll definitely find out," Derek replied, kissing her face.

"Alright, we'll see how imperfect you can be," she said.

But her companion had already resumed his usual serious demeanor.

"Dawn is soon," he whispered.

"Already? That was quick."

"It's time for you to go home. I'll come tomorrow if you don't mind. We could have dinner at that restaurant," Derek pointed towards one of the hills.

"I don't mind," Megan replied, looking forward to their next meeting.

"I'll be there at 10:00 p.m." he said, releasing her from his embrace.

"Great!"

"Let's go, I'll walk you home."

She embraced him around the neck and gently kissed him. She didn't want to leave him at all, and he didn't want to let her go. But he knew it was time…

When the girl found herself in her bedroom, she understood what it meant to be the happiest person in the world, because that's exactly how she felt at that moment. She discovered what love is. Love that fills every cell of the body. This intense emotion seemed to squeeze her heart so tightly that it was hard to breathe. For Derek, she was now ready to go to the end of the world and back again. And now, she very well understood what her mother meant before she moved to America. Megan's ears echoed her words, "Baby, I know it's a very difficult choice right now, but one day you'll understand me. There's nothing more powerful in life than love. When it comes—everything changes: the values, the meaning of being." Megan was amazed at how quickly and unconditionally one can fall in love with someone, how in one moment everything changes, and there's no turning back.

It was difficult to fall asleep. Thoughts overwhelmed her, emotions ran high, but she needed to rest at least a little before the trip to the islands tomorrow.

*****

She managed to sleep only a couple of hours before the alarm went off and it was time to get ready. Megan thought about the unfortunate day they chose for this trip. But somehow, the usual predictability of life didn't apply here.

Nobody could have known in advance that on this sleepless night she would find the love of her life.

She quickly washed up, combed her gorgeous hair, dressed warmly, and went down to the kitchen to drink a double shot of strong coffee. Warren and Glenn were just finishing breakfast.

"Good morning, Megan," the couple said in unison.

"Good morning," she said with a smile and reached for the coffee.

"Aren't you going to have breakfast?" Glenn asked in surprise.

"No, I don't want to. I'll just have some cookies," murmured the sleep-deprived girl.

"Are you feeling okay?" Glenn asked worriedly.

"Yes, I'm fine. Just didn't sleep much. Insomnia. It happens sometimes."

"If you want, we can stop by a pharmacy today and get you some calming drops; they'll help with the insomnia."

"Thanks, Glenn, I think that's a good idea. We can stop by on the way back."

"Well, are you ready? If so, let's go," Warren said cheerfully, getting up from the table.

"Yes, we can head out," Megan replied.

Sitting in Warren's cozy car, she again immersed herself in thoughts about Derek.

Arriving at the port, they saw Duncan and Craig there.

"Hi, Megan," Craig greeted her joyously.

"Craig, Duncan, it's nice to see you both!" she said.

"The weather is wonderful today, so the trip should be fantastic," Craig observed.

Leaving their cars in the parking lot, the group chatted and headed towards the dock, where a boat was prepared. Fifteen minutes later, everyone was aboard the vessel heading to Kirkwall, located on the Orkney Islands.

"Ladies and gentlemen, welcome aboard!" Craig announced playfully, mimicking a sea captain, wanting to catch Megan's attention. Spreading a blanket in his hands, he continued, "If you get cold during the journey, you can always cover yourselves with the blankets under your seats," with these words, he carefully covered the girl's shoulders.

"Thank you, captain, you're very kind!" she thanked him with a smile.

The day was clear and sunny. The sky was cloudless. But Megan knew that despite the good weather, it would definitely be cold on the way due to the headwind.

"How long will it take us to get there?" she asked.

"About an hour," Duncan replied.

The company was made up of interesting conversationalists, and time flew by unnoticed.

From Kirkwall, they began their exploration of the island. Megan couldn't get enough of the beauty that unfolded before her eyes. Magnificent cliffs of various shapes and heights extended deep into the sea. The delightful sandy beaches invited peace and solitude. She couldn't have imagined such a variety of landscapes in this area. Moving from one place to another, they eventually arrived at the famous Ring of Brodgar. This ring consisted of 27 megalithic stones and had been here for several thousand years. It was unknown who built it and for what purpose—whether it was the Celts or those before them, there were no answers to these questions.

"Originally, the ring had about 60 stones, the rest hadn't survived to our time," Warren began. "Legends say that for many centuries, sacrifices were made on an altar situated in the center of the megalithic circle to appease various gods. Locals say that at first, virgins and children were offered as sacrifices, and in later times — animals. Nowadays, this place is just a tourist attraction, listed as a UNESCO World Heritage Site."

"Such gigantic stones," Megan exclaimed in admiration.

"And how many terrifying stories they hold in their memory," Duncan said. "I really like this place; it's definitely filled with mystique."

Craig also contributed, "The local legend says, once every four years, according to the Celtic calendar, on the night of November 11th to 12th, a unique astronomical event occurs. Stars and planets align in a special order, creating a connection with the altar within the ancient stone circle. It's said that if you lie on the altar at midnight, you can momentarily connect with cosmic forces and receive answers to the most important questions about the past and the future. However, the altar must first be sprinkled with the blood of those seeking knowledge."

"This is the first time I'm hearing such a legend, Craig. Did you just make it up to scare Megan?" Warren asked, laughing.

But Duncan supported the storyteller, "I've heard about this from some locals as well."

"And does the belief actually work?" Megan asked Craig, surprised.

"I have no idea, nor the desire to test it. Many tell the legend, but no one has ever named a single person who received any information from the cosmos while lying on this altar. I think it's just as much of a fairy tale as the blooming fern. Our region loves mysterious stories. Point out any mysterious place, and immediately a new tale is invented, giving it the utmost mysticism," he replied.

"I completely agree with you, Craig," Duncan said. "If we were to go to the sea now and set up another stone circle, even if it's smaller than this one, by tomorrow a story would be born about some sea monster that built its altar on land to communicate with the Universe. And by next year, this myth would be known across the north of Scotland."

Warren also eagerly joined the conversation, "Megan, Scots are special people, remember, it's only in our country that the Loch Ness Monster lives. Just think about it, nowhere else in the world, in none of the tens of thousands of lakes on Earth, does any creature like this exist, but in Scotland, it does, and what a creature it is! Do you know how many tales are associated with it? All you have to do is visit any bookshop and you'll find dozens of books with countless myths about this being. During the boat ride on the lake, they'll tell you at least ten different stories related to the Nessie monster within an hour."

Megan was impressed. People had invented so many stories about a single lake inhabitant! For a moment, she wondered what she actually knew about the most popular, albeit possibly fictional, Scottish creature.

"Could you tell me more about this monster?" she said, addressing Warren. "I saw something about it on TV, but I can't remember what it was."

"I'd be happy to share all I know. In the lake itself, Loch Ness was formed at the end of the Ice Age, about 10,000 years ago. Its water is murky and black due to the abundance of peat, but it is very deep and surrounded by steep cliffs. Until recently, before tourist paths were laid, it was an impassable and inaccessible place. Hence, the most popular theory is that the Loch Ness Monster is a descendant of a surviving dinosaur. Some scientists believe the lake is connected to the sea through underground tunnels and that several dinosaurs could have survived thanks to this. There's no confirmation that there's more than one, but it's unlikely that the creature could have survived alone. According to ancient legends, Roman legionnaires were the first to tell of this monster. All known animals were immortalized by local inhabitants on stones. There was only one animal the Romans couldn't identify — a huge seal with a very long neck. In the sixth century AD, a certain water beast appears in the chronicles, but then all mentions of it disappear until the late nineteenth century. People living near Loch Ness today remember being forbidden to swim as children, because of a hellish creature with a horse's head that drags people into the depths and eats them there."

"You're telling too many horror stories," Craig said.

"What do you think about this creature? You probably know a lot about it too?" Megan asked him.

"I prefer the theory that the Loch Ness Monster is a vision that appears under the influence of hallucinogenic gases. The lake is located on a huge earth crust fault. This fault facilitates small earthquakes, and the release of gases from underneath can cause hallucinations in people. However, it's unclear why these hallucinations are similar among different people. Or perhaps it's a supernatural entity that penetrates our world through astral tunnels."

Duncan continued the theme, "Also, Loch Ness and the creature living in it are a local attraction that draws many tourists. And that brings substantial money to hoteliers and the city administration. It's quite possible that all the tales about the monster are made up to keep visitors interested in the place. Tourists will visit the lake in hopes of seeing an unknown creature to humanity, meanwhile leaving quite a sum of money behind."

"Regardless, for several centuries, scientists have been trying to get to the truth of whether something large and unexplored lives in Loch Ness; locals and tourists try to photograph it... But so far, there's not a single convincing explanation for this phenomenon," Warren concluded his story.

"Yes, Scots are indeed unique people," Megan said.

The group members dispersed in different directions around the stone circle, examining the ancient megalithic slabs. Megan approached one of the megaliths and ran her hand over its rough, cold surface. At that moment, a strong wind blew from the sea, and strands of hair blew onto her face. Craig, who stood beside her, carefully moved the strands away from her face. This gesture seemed quite intimate to her. Unexpectedly, out of nowhere, a black raven flew between them, brushing the young man's face with its wing.

"Damn bird," he snapped, stepping back slightly startled.

It was so sudden that they each got a fright. The raven made a few circles above their heads and flew away.

"I've noticed that these ravens are very bold around here. One constantly circles around Castle Mal. Once, it even landed on my hand when I was trying to pick flowers in the field. These birds scare me," Megan said, looking disdainfully after the departing raven.

"Pay no attention to them, Megan. They're just birds. Maybe they're going through some kind of nesting frenzy right now, who knows," Craig said, annoyed at being robbed of an intimate moment with the girl.

"You're right. It's just a bird. But it's very unpleasant when it suddenly appears everywhere I go," Megan sighed, stepping away from the giant stone.

"Guys, come here!" called Glenn, spreading a picnic blanket on the grass outside the circle.

The diligent hostess had prepared everything for a picnic in advance. She placed a checkered basket in the center of the makeshift table, from which she took out cheese, sandwiches, apples, and a bottle of wine, which Warren immediately opened. Pouring the contents into glasses, he handed each person their share.

"Here's to a good, warm day! Such weather is rare around here," Duncan said.

They clinked glasses. After taking a sip of wine, Megan noticed a raven sitting nearby on the grass, watching them attentively. Glenn followed her friend's gaze and said, "It's staring at us so strangely; it's probably hungry."

With these words, she pinched off a piece of bread from a sandwich and extended it towards the bird. The raven shifted its gaze from Megan to Glenn, looked at her intently, but stayed put. Then, she threw the bread towards it, thinking the feathered creature was simply afraid to come too close to people. But it simply looked at the offered treat then fixed its gaze back on Megan.

"Try feeding it; it's looking at you. Maybe it will take food from your hands," Glenn suggested.

"Indeed, perhaps yours tastes better," added Duncan with a playful smile, and he winked at Megan, as if teasing Glenn.

"I don't want to, I'm scared of it," the girl said, looking at the raven in terror.

"But this is a different raven. Not the one from Castle Mal. It wouldn't have flown so far from home. Try giving it some bread," Glenn persisted.

"Alright. Only because you're asking. But I really don't like these birds being near me," Megan said, displeased.

She pinched off a piece of sandwich and cautiously extended it to the bird. She was scared it might peck her hand or attack her. The raven looked at her intently for a long time, then approached slowly and carefully, taking the bread from her hand...never taking its eyes off her face.

"Look at that, you're more to its liking than Glenn," Craig laughed.

"Megan, maybe you did inherit something from Margaret after all? See how the creatures come to you! Can you, by chance, hear its thoughts? What's on its mind?" Warren joked.

"No, I can't hear them! And I wouldn't want to be able to," she said, feeling a bit relieved that she wasn't bitten.

The thought that the raven wouldn't harm her greatly calmed her fear of it.

For the next fifteen minutes, each took turns offering food to the unexpected guest, but it accepted treats from no one other than Megan. After some time, it lost interest in the crowd and flew away, leaving them to continue their picnic.

Having fully enjoyed and admired the local scenery, the travelers returned to the boat, and soon landed back at the pier from where their sea journey had begun. After saying goodbye, they headed home. Megan was thrilled about her day and eagerly awaited her meeting with Derek. At dinner with Glenn and Warren, she only drank tea, claiming she wasn't hungry. She didn't want to mention the dinner invitation. Thanking her friends for a wonderful day, she wished them a good night and went to her room.

11
Uncertainty

Ensuring the corridor was empty, at precisely 10pm., she left the castle. He was standing in the same spot as always, waiting for her. Black trousers and a black shirt made him almost invisible in the dark. Megan was unaccustomed to seeing Derek dressed like this; he always wore a kilt before.

"You look great in that style. I like it," she said admiringly.

"Thanks for the compliment, you look great too."

Derek embraced her and they began climbing the hill to the restaurant.

"How was your day? What did you do?"

"We went to the Orkney Islands. Such a beautiful place. Scotland is full of surprises. In just a few days, I've come to love this country. I don't understand why I hadn't visited earlier. You've been to the islands, right?"

"Yes, several times. I like it there too. I think those places have a special allure, even magic: tranquil silence, enchanting nature, and powerful energy from the ancient stone giants," his eyes lit up with the warm glow of memories.

"And what about you? Have you traveled a lot?" asked Derek.

"Yes, quite a bit. My mom loved warm countries, so we often traveled in winter, sometimes in summer, to lie on the beach and bask in the sunshine. So, you could call me a holiday expert," she said with feigned seriousness. "We spent a lot of time in Cuba, flew to Thailand, but Italy has touched my soul the most. Oh, the emotions, passion...rhythm! And all that coexists with tranquility."

Megan's face lit by a tender smile, as she became lost in thought. "And how do you feel about traveling?"

"I have visited all the capitals of Europe. So, I understand your feelings about Italy, even though I'm not a big fan of it."

"To be honest, I'm terribly afraid of flying; I always feel more comfortable on the ground than in the sky or on water. That's why I don't really like long-distance travel. Our flights to Thailand and Cuba were tough for me. Aren't you afraid of flying?" Megan asked.

"No, not at all. Actually, you could even say I rather enjoy the process of flying."

"Lucky you!" Megan said with a hint of envy.

"Indeed," he remarked with a slight note of sarcasm.

They entered a small but cozy establishment. The place was furnished with lacquered tables covered with white-and red-checkered tablecloths, and massive chairs upholstered in rich mahogany fabric. Warm, subdued light filled the room, emanating from candlesticks attached to the wooden walls. Pleasant music played from the back of the hall, creating a unique atmosphere of comfort and charm. The few guests at the restaurant were mainly locals. They looked over the newcomers from head to toe and, taking them for tourists, quickly lost interest.

A friendly waiter greeted the couple. He led them to a small table by the window, where they could enjoy each other's company without interruption.

"Could I recommend something to you?" the waiter asked?

Megan and Derek exchanged glances and understood each other without words. The girl happily left the management of the evening to her companion.

"Bring us a bottle of your best red wine," replied Derek.

The waiter took the order and left the guests, returning a few minutes later with a bottle of exquisite Italian Barolo.

The lovers continued their conversation.

"I still don't know the most important thing about you!" Derek suddenly exclaimed. With silence as a response, he continued, "I don't know your food preferences. Being a pro in the restaurant business, I assume it's not easy to please you."

"Actually, no. I'm not picky about food. At my establishment, I usually eat whatever the chef prepares. When on vacation with my mom, we always tried local dishes. And having arrived at Castle Mal and getting acquainted with the local customs, I've become a real fan of your cuisine. The way they prepare game and fish here is wonderful; I really liked it. And what about you? What do you like?"

"In that aspect, we're alike; I'm also not very fussy about food."

At that moment, the waiter returned. He quickly but carefully filled their glasses with rich red liquid. After arranging the meat dishes with a side of potatoes and vegetables, he wished them a pleasant meal and left.

"To our first dinner together?" Derek proposed, with a raised glass at Megan.

"To our first real date!" she added.

After taking a sip of wine, they noted the waiter's excellent choice and started their meal.

"How was your day?" she asked Derek.

"Quite ordinary, nothing special. Who did you go to the islands with?" he unexpectedly asked, changing the subject.

"With my cousins, Glenn – Warren's wife, and his friend."

"What friend?" Derek asked a bit tensely.

The girl shrugged, "I don't know, a long-time friend of Warren. He happened to be at the restaurant where we had our family dinner. That's where we were introduced. Are you jealous?" Megan asked teasingly.

"No, just curious," he smiled back.

"His name is Craig, and he works for a shipping company. When he found out we were going to the islands, he decided to join us. Quite an interesting guy, easy to talk to."

"Interesting..." Derek slowly repeated, cocking his right eyebrow.

"Why do you look like that? He's interesting to talk to, nothing more," Megan laughed, pleasantly flattered by Derek's slight jealousy.

"I'm glad it's nothing more," he said with a smile, looking straight into her eyes.

There was an awkward pause between them for a moment.

"Have you had any serious relationships with women before? Like, a long-term commitment or marriage?" Megan calmly asked, trying to hide her inner turmoil.

He paused before answering, his face once again becoming an impenetrable mask, making it impossible to read any emotions.

"I've had a serious and long-term relationship…" he continued to look into her eyes as he spoke.

Derek was hesitant, afraid to accidentally hurt Megan's feelings. He chose his words with utmost care. However, the pace at which she asked her questions threw him off balance.

"How long ago did this relationship end?"

"A long time ago."

"Did it cause you pain and suffering?"

"Not the relationship itself, but the consequences."

"Do you feel better now?"

"Definitely," he replied, now smiling.

"Do you still love her?"

He watched Megan closely, noticing a flicker of fear in her eyes. She feared his answer to this question, afraid he might say "yes," and he understood that.

"Too many years have passed…" he said slowly. "Let's leave the past behind and talk about us instead. I feel like I've known you all my life. Do you feel the same?" he asked calmly, with a slight smile and a squint in his eyes.

"I do," she replied, satisfied with his answers.

Derek raised his glass, "Then let's drink to that."

The tension at their table eased, allowing them to comfortably continue their dinner.

"Madam, now that you've extracted all my secrets, it's your turn to answer my questions. Tell me about your personal life. I'm eager to hear," he said with a smile.

"There's not much to tell. I was in a relationship for several years, but it didn't feel like the sincere and true love portrayed in movies and novels. We parted ways and remained friends. And now there's you in my life, and I'm very happy about it."

"I'm also very happy we met," Derek said.

Taking a sip of drink, he added, "This wine is delightful! If it weren't for this decor, I'd believe I was in Italy! But we'll talk about that later. Have you decided on the fate of the factory and the castle?"

"Yes, I've made my decision known to the family. Warren will manage everything, after all he has experience in this business and he's a McKenzie. Honestly, managing such a large and unfamiliar production was never of interest to me. I understand that my grandfather probably hadn't foreseen this scenario. He wanted me to take full control and devote my life to the ancient family business. Unfortunately, I don't feel the same passion and enthusiasm for the distillery that I do for the London restaurant. It's just not my cup of tea."

"If that's what you really want, then it's probably the best solution. When are you leaving for London?" Derek asked casually, taking another sip of wine to dull his anxiety as he awaited her answer.

"I think I'll extend my summer vacation here a bit longer. It's been a while since I had a holiday. It's the perfect opportunity to make up for lost time."

Derek breathed a sigh of relief and said, "So, we'll have more time to spend together."

"Yes, I'll have a chance to learn more about you," Megan smiled.

"I thought you knew enough about me," Derek said with feigned surprise, before revealing a genuine smile.

"On the one hand, yes, but on the other, it seems I know almost nothing about you. You still remain a mystery to me."

"Does that frighten you?"

"Not anymore, but curiosity prevails," laughed Megan.

"Everything in its own time. I think you'll find the answers to your questions soon."

"I hope so."

After dinner, they went for a walk to the sea. This had become their favorite spot, where they would sit on a large boulder, embracing each other, and talking the night away. As always, she returned to the castle just before dawn, first alone, and now with her beloved.

Weeks passed, and Derek spent the night in Megan's room more and more frequently, where they passionately made love. Sometimes, without warning, he would appear in her bedroom in the middle of the night. Megan couldn't understand these strange appearances and disappearances, but she gave herself to him with all her soul, body, and heart. Their love for each other grew stronger by the day, and the girl could no longer imagine her life without him. Before dawn, her lover always left, leaving her alone with heavy thoughts about how time passed but nothing changed. He remained just as mysterious and enigmatic as ever, yet at the same time, he was the dearest and most beloved person in the world to her.

*****

Three months had passed since Megan arrived at Castle Mal. As a perfectionist, she always required clear direction on how to proceed with her life and what actions to take. The situation she found herself in threw her off rhythm. Derek, occupied with his confidential job, wasn't ready to accompany her to London, and no one could say when his commitments would end. Megan realized that she needed to return home, yet she couldn't leave her loved one behind. Every day, she convinced herself that tomorrow she would find a way out of this loop and make a decision about her future. However, each new "tomorrow" passed without resolution. Megan waited for Derek to suggest something, to take some responsibility for their relationship and future, but he remained silent. Then one day, her phone rang.

"Honey, how are you? Are you in London yet?"

"Hi, Mom, I'm still at Castle Mal."

"What are you doing there for so long? Did you like it so much that you decided to stay forever?"

"No, I just took a long vacation. I'm enjoying northern Scotland, it's very beautiful here, and I want to stay a bit longer," the girl answered.

"Dear, you've been there for three months. What more is there to see? You can explore the entire north from end to end in just a few days. I can't understand you. It's a godforsaken place, where life has stopped, and there's no development. In my opinion, there's nothing to do there for more than a week," Arline said, puzzled, unaware of what was really happening with her daughter.

"Everyone has their own opinion. Tell me how you're doing instead," Megan decided to change the subject.

"Honey, I've missed you. You haven't visited us for a long time, and I really want to see you. Come back to London. Ted and I will be there in five days."

Megan was stunned listening to her mother. Leave Derek and go to London in five days? She wasn't ready for that.

"Have you already bought the tickets?" she asked nervously.

"Yes, dear, we have," Arline's voice was filled with genuine joy.

"Mom why don't you come here to Castle Mal? It's your home, after all."

"Megan, I have unpleasant memories of that house. I don't want to go back there. And your grandfather would turn in his grave if I stepped foot in Castle Mal," Arline sighed heavily.

"But what happened between the two of you in the past? He didn't even want to reconcile with his only daughter before he died. There must have been a good reason."

There was a brief silence on the line.

"Mom, can you hear me?"

"Baby, this isn't a conversation for over the phone. We'll talk when we meet."

Megan suggested enthusiastically, "I have an idea! Let's meet in Edinburgh? I plan to return to London a bit later. Sam keeps in touch with me daily; everything's fine at the restaurant and there's no need for me to be there all the time. You know that over the years we've streamlined operations so much that now, for the first time in my life, I can afford to take a longer break."

"Well, if that's how you feel, I have no objections. I'm very fond of Edinburgh and I wouldn't mind spending a few days there. I think Ted will like this idea. We could stop in London for a day first. I'll check in with Sam and see how things are going there. And the next day, we'll take a train to Scotland," Arline clearly liked the plan.

"Great! I'd really appreciate it if you popped into the restaurant to check how things are going."

"Megan, are you sure everything's okay? Or is there something I don't know about? This whole story with your extended holiday seems very strange to me. Have you met a man there? Are you in love? Be honest with me," Arline asked anxiously, terrified at the thought of her only daughter staying forever away from civilization because of some Highlander.

"Don't worry, Mum. I just like it here. I need a little rest and relaxation after all the hustle and bustle of London," Megan convincingly answered.

"But I know you! You wouldn't be able to sit still for even a day without something to do. And here we're talking about months," Arline disapproved.

"I guess I'm just very tired. Working non-stop caught up with me in the end. You know, I hadn't taken a real break in ages. Well, the time has finally come to make up for all those missed holidays."

"Okay, whatever you say. I'll look for apartments in Edinburgh today and give you the address. We'll talk in a couple of days. Love you, sweetie, and can't wait to see you."

"Love you too. Hugs. Say hi to Ted."

"Will do!"

The trip to Edinburgh appealed more to Megan than returning to London. Going to London meant leaving Scotland for a while and resuming her usual routine, but the time for that hadn't come yet. She would have to tell Derek, as well as Glenn and Warren, that she would be leaving for a short while. She saw her friend from the hall window and headed outside.

"Megan! Look at how beautifully the roses have grown, they are even more beautiful this year than the last," her friend admired, gazing at her own garden.

"Glenn, everything you plant grows beautifully! You have green fingers."

"Thank you. I really enjoy the process when you plant a seed and watch it grow stronger day by day. Eventually, it turns into a work of art," Glenn said passionately.

Megan shrugged, as she couldn't quite appreciate the full joy of watching a seed or root sprout. She had never planted anything in her life.

"I just spoke to my mother. I'm going to Edinburgh on Saturday, and she's coming there with her husband for a few days. I'll be with them for five days then I'll come back."

"I'm glad you'll see your mom! She wouldn't like to come to Castle Mal, would she? That would be great!"

"No, she doesn't like this place at all."

"Pity, I don't know how it's possible not to love it. I've grown so attached to you, Megan, that I find it hard to imagine you being away for five days," Glenn said, hugging her friend.

"But sooner or later the day will come when I'll have to return to London and resume my usual life," Megan said with a sad smile.

"I'm not even ready to think about that yet. I'll be visiting you often then," laughed Glenn.

"Come over, you're always welcome."

"Let's cut these roses and take them to Malcolm's crypt."

"Right now?" Megan asked, startled.

"Why not?"

"I'm scared to go there without male accompaniment. Warren has escorted me a couple of times, but even with him, I was frightened. And you're suggesting we go there, just the two of us?"

"Let's call Gregor."

"He left for the distillery an hour ago."

"Did he? I didn't even notice he was gone."

"The main quality of Gregor is his inconspicuousness. He never seems to be around even when he is, making him always seem absent," Megan laughed.

Glenn also laughed and said, "You're absolutely right. Oh, look, Warren is coming, he's early today."

Warren didn't come alone; he was with his friend.

Craig greeted both women with a friendly kiss in turn, "Hello there, happy to see you both!"

Since their introduction, he had invited Megan to the movies and dinner twice. And twice she had declined. She felt very awkward around him. She knew about his clear interest in her, but she didn't want to conflict with Derek, or give Craig false hope.

"Hi, Craig. What an unexpected but pleasant surprise," Megan sincerely said.

"I ran into him in Thurso and suggested he join us for dinner," Warren joined the conversation.

"Good thinking. Megan and I have been quite bored these last few days. You're always at work, and we have no one else to talk to. Just each other, day in, day out," Glenn jokingly told her husband.

"I'm always ready to keep you company. We can get together again and go somewhere, like the last time we went to the islands," Craig suggested.

"I'm leaving for Edinburgh on Saturday for a few days. My mom is coming and I'm going to meet her."

"You'll come back here afterward, right?" Craig asked hopefully.

"Yes, I'll come back. I've decided to spend some more time here."

"We won't let her go to London for long," Warren cheerfully said. "We've become so close living under the same roof that it's hard to imagine what Glenn and I will do without her."

"Let's go inside; I'll hurry the cook with dinner and we can start earlier today," Megan suggested.

"Sure. We can start with a glass of whiskey by the fireplace," Warren proposed.

"Let's do that," Glenn agreed.

While Megan went to the kitchen, they settled in the living room. Glenn and Warren in armchairs, and Craig on the sofa. Megan returned and sat next to him.

"Craig, how are you? How's work? It's been a while since I've seen you," Megan asked with interest.

"Nothing new. Work's the same as always. Everything's fine with the family, thank God! I've just been a bit bored with the monotony of life. But tell me, what do you do here all day?"

"In the morning, I'm almost always on the phone with London. Solving various issues; basically working. Then Glenn and I chat, and afterwards, I go to the library to read. It's pretty much the same routine every day. It's the first time my life has been like this. But I'm not complaining. The main thing is that there's something to do," she said with a smile.

"A day packed with activity," Craig chuckled.

"Indeed! I'm really looking forward to this trip to Edinburgh; It'll give me a chance to unwind completely."

"I've been to Edinburgh a few times. It's a very beautiful city. You'd want to return again and again."

"That's true, it's so unique, amazing, I would say. My grandfather and I met there a few times when I was a teenager. Mom would see me off to the train in London, and Grandpa would pick me up at the railway station in Edinburgh. I feel like you can never get tired of that city."

"I think everyone would agree with that," said Craig.

"By the way, Megan, I saw Duncan today," Warren joined the conversation. "He sends his regards and asked when you will finally come to visit them. He and Grandfather would be delighted to see you. I suggest we organize a family dinner at their place as soon as you return from your trip."

Megan was pleased that her relationship with the family had developed in such a warm way. Over these months, she has grown fond of Alaric, who reminded her of her grandfather, and the lively Duncan, with whom it was always fun. Therefore, she responded very positively to her cousin's suggestion, "That's a great idea! Send them my warm regards."

Warren smiled, "I also told my brother not to worry about your infrequent visits, and explained that as soon as you finish reading the entire Castle Mal library, you'll move to the Castle Raven library. Given the rate at which you devour books, I think that's about to happen. How many have you read during this time? Two hundred?"

"No, about twenty-five, I think," Megan laughed.

"That's some speed! I don't read half that in a year," Craig was amazed.

"Of course, Craig, you work all day. You're not going to read in the office in front of your colleagues. And I'm on vacation, so I have time," she said with a smile.

"By the way, I also have a large library at home. Once you're done with these two, you can move to mine," Craig offered cheerfully.

"Thank you. I think that might happen in a couple of decades. If I stay here until retirement and do nothing else, I could manage two libraries, reading twelve hours a day," Megan reasoned with laughter.

"I'd be happy if you stayed here for a couple more decades. By the way, how's your interaction with the birds going? Still as successful? Warren mentioned that one of the ravens has become your companion and follows you everywhere."

"Yes, it's true! At first, I was afraid of it, but then I got used to it. I feed it occasionally, so it looks for me everywhere. If

I'm in the study, it sits by the window; if I'm in the bedroom, it's by another window. Well, not always, of course. But it definitely spends a couple of hours a day around me. It's quite funny," Megan said, surprising herself that she had become friends with a bird.

"It's her biggest fan," Warren said, laughing. "Don't forget, Megan: we're responsible for those we've tamed."

"Wise words, indeed. I'll go see if dinner is ready," she said, getting up from the couch.

"Don't get up, Megan; I'll go hurry Finella along. I'm already hungry," Glenn said, quickly standing up and heading to the kitchen.

At that moment, the phone rang. Warren excused himself and walked over to the grand staircase to answer it. Meanwhile, Craig turned to Megan and, seizing the opportunity to be alone with her, asked, "Are you avoiding me?"

"Of course not!"

"I've asked you out twice, and you turned me down."

"I'm sorry, it was just bad timing," Megan said, at a loss for how to properly respond to his question without hurting his feelings.

"So, you're saying there's still a chance? I just need to pick the right time?" he asked hopefully.

As they were sitting close, Craig tenderly brushed a strand of hair from her face, much like Derek often did. He leaned in closely, intending to kiss her. Megan quickly leaned her head back to avoid the kiss.

"Craig, I'm sorry, we're not alone... I'm just not ready..." she began to explain hurriedly, unsure of how to defuse this awkward situation.

"Sorry. I understand. I won't rush you," he replied.

Glenn returned to the room, not noticing the tension that had lingered between Megan and Craig. Her appearance helped to ease the atmosphere.

Over dinner, both the girl and the young man tried to avoid eye contact. They were both upset by the uncomfortable situation that had occurred in the room, but tried their best to act naturally, as if nothing had happened. Without waiting for dessert, Craig excused himself by saying he had promised a friend to help with something, said goodbye to everyone and swiftly left.

"Meg, is everything all right? It seemed to me that Craig was upset about something," Warren asked with concern.

"I don't know. I didn't notice. Maybe he has some personal problems; who knows! I'm going to my room; I want to have an early night tonight, you don't mind?"

"Good night."

After saying goodbye to her relatives, Megan walked up to her room. She was tormented by a sense of guilt towards Craig, for possibly leading him on and giving false hope. She imagined how rejected he must now be feeling. Reason told her that it wasn't her fault. But to feel and to understand are two different things, and at that moment, they were battling inside her. The girl wanted to be alone as soon as possible to think over the day's events: the call from her mother, preparations for Edinburgh, Craig...

Entering her room, she was greatly surprised to find Derek there. He sat in the chair by the window, legs crossed, arms folded over his chest. He was once again wearing his trousers and shirt, all in black.

"Derek!? You scared me! I didn't expect to see you so early."

"Who were you expecting to see here? Craig?" he remarked, unable to contain his sarcasm.

"Did you see him? He joined us for dinner tonight."

"Yes, I saw him; he just left, we passed each other a couple of meters apart. Why did he come?" Derek inquired.

"I told you before, he's Warren's friend, and he just came over for a friendly dinner."

"I see. I think he's very interested in you."

"What gives you that idea?"

"I don't know... male intuition."

Megan had never seen Derek so agitated and tense, as if something was tormenting him inside. She decided to change the subject to find out what was really happening with him.

"Why did you come so early? It's only 9:20."

He was staring into space, lost in his thoughts, not hearing the question.

"Derek!"

"Yes, Megan?" he looked at her as if he had just woken up.

"You've never come this early before. Is everything okay?"

"I got off work at 5 today and couldn't wait to see you," he replied calmly.

"I'm really happy you're here. I missed you."

"I missed you too," he said, getting up and putting his arms around her before kissing her gently.

"My mom called today. She and Ted are coming, we've arranged to spend a few days together in Edinburgh. I'm going there on Saturday."

"And then?" he asked tensely.

"I'll come back."

Each evening he spent with her, he feared hearing about her return to London. Today, he especially didn't want to broach the subject. He tried to steer the conversation away from it, but now realized it was inevitable.

"Okay, I'll be waiting for you. What are your plans for tomorrow, and what did you do today?" he tried to guide the conversation in a direction he deemed appropriate.

"Same as usual. Work, Glenn, reading. Honestly, I'm starting to get bored with this lifestyle. My life in England was always so eventful and dynamic. I miss that. I don't know what to do with myself here. How long will this continue?! More precisely, how much longer can I take it?" Megan was depressed. She didn't want to rake over all this again, but it was imperative for her to set her limits; she couldn't wait in uncertainty forever.

Derek closed his eyes and sighed heavily, "Megan, I completely understand what you're waiting for from me. And I too want us to spend more time together. Not only at night but also during the day. But I can't give you that right now. Not because I don't want to, but because I can't, due to... certain circumstances.

"Derek, you say you love me, but we don't go out. We don't go anywhere together because everything is closed at night. You never call me. You don't have days off. We've been together for more than three months, but nothing has changed. There's no development in the relationship. It's all very strange and I'm plagued by various doubts and anxiety. Please understand I can't stay here forever. Sooner or later, I'll have to go back to London. What will happen to us then?"

Megan was filled with despair and hopelessness as she laid these grievances on Derek.

"I'm sorry I'm causing you such discomfort. I understand perfectly well how you feel. You've got every reason to be angry with me. I need to know, in spite of all this, do you love me?"

"Of course, I do, but what does that change?"

"You've never told me that before."

"I'm afraid — afraid of uncertainty and that you might hurt me."

"The last thing I want to do is hurt you, Megan. I love you. Give me a little time. Just one or two months, no more. I promise you everything will change. You'll get answers to all your questions."

His eyes were filled with so much sadness that Megan's heart clenched in pain.

"Fine," she said with a note of resignation.

Derek hugged her tightly, feeling burdened himself by all the half-truths and deceit in which he has lived these past months. That night, he was the most passionate and tender lover in the world. Megan felt so good and peaceful because he was there. In such moments, she forgot all her fears concerning him. Beside her, was the most faithful and loving of all men. She believed in the sincerity of his feelings and knew that he truly loved her as deeply as she loved him. But she needed to wait another a little longer, as Derek had asked her to.

They lay in bed, embracing. Megan looked at the clock — dawn was near, and it was time for him to leave again. Where? And why exactly at this time? These questions remained unanswered.

12

Story of the Past

Megan packed her suitcase, filled with a sense of joy in anticipation of the trip. Despite feeling sad about leaving Derek for five days, especially since their maximum separation over the past three months was no more than 24 hours, it did not overshadow the upcoming meeting with her mom, whom she's missed so much. She was eager to be among the crowd and immerse herself in the life of the capital.

Warren and Glenn accompanied her to the station. The journey to Edinburgh took seven hours, but time flew by unnoticed. She admired the spectacular views from the train window. The landscapes were stunning in their diversity, changing one after another. Part of the route passed along the North Sea, with its magnificent sandy beaches and mountains, dotted with pink heather. Only in the north of Scotland can one see fairy-tale pink mountains, beautiful valleys with rivers and streams, pastures, and flocks of sheep that provide wool is to produce national clothing and accessories. It was impossible to get tired of the scenery. Love for these lands and for Derek filled Megan's heart. After their conversation a few days ago, she decided to stay at Castle Mal for another two months. She hoped that something would really change and there would be some certainty for the future. She also looked forward to meeting her mom, remembering their life in London, working at the restaurant, their joint vacations... Why had she never been interested in the reason behind her mom's argument with her grandfather? Why hadn't he forgiven her even before his death? Why was her mom so categorically refusing to come to the house where she was born and raised? So many "whys" swirled in her head. Well, perhaps it was time to uncover the family secret. Her mom promised to tell her everything. With these thoughts, lulled by the monotonous rumbling of the wheels, the girl dozed off.

The train arrived at Waverley Central Station. She took her suitcase and headed for the exit. Arline and Ted were supposed to arrive in three hours.

Megan decided to leave her suitcase in the apartment, situated two hundred meters from the station, and go for a stroll around the old town. She planned to return by the time the train from London would arrive.

Free from luggage, she crossed Princess Street and climbed up to the historical center of the capital. Edinburgh continued to amaze and impress, with the beauty of its streets and architectural buildings. Finding herself in its very heart, Megan felt like she was in a mythical world. Bagpipes could be heard everywhere. Shops were abundant in souvenirs and a variety of national woolen clothes were sold in a range of colors for tourists. The weather was nice. Megan walked the entire Royal Mile — from the royal castle to the end, where the Parliament and Holyrood Hill were located. At first, she thought of climbing to the top again, as she did several years ago, but looking at her watch, she gave up on that idea. The ascent to one of the highest viewing platforms took about an hour. Turning back, she passed by Holyrood Palace and headed to the station to meet her long-awaited relatives, enjoying the feeling of being among a large crowd of people along the way. She had missed this atmosphere a lot lately. The girl was once again in the environment she had lived in for years. If Derek offers her a chance of a serious relationship, they could move to Edinburgh, if he didn't want to leave Scotland. She considered the possibility of regular train trips to London for business. Moreover, she could often visit Castle Mal and Thurso, thus maintaining a connection with both sides of her life. Her man had nothing holding him back there. He says he has no family.

Edinburgh beckoned the girl; it seemed to her the epicenter of art, culture, creativity, and beauty, while remaining a dynamic and active city. It was a place where she could find happiness and complete life satisfaction. Dreams and wonders came alive here at every step. Engrossed in her thoughts, Megan didn't immediately notice the arrival of the train from London. Five minutes later, she saw her mother and Ted rushing towards her.

"Mom!"

"Honey!" Arline wrapped her in a tight embrace and smothered her with kisses. "I missed you so much, my little girl!"

"I missed you too," Megan sincerely said.

Freeing herself from her mother's embrace, she hugged her stepfather.

"Hi, Ted! I'm happy to see you again."

"Likewise, Megan!" he affectionately patted her head, slightly ruffling her hair.

"Long time no see. You can never find the time to come down to the States for a week or two."

"You're right, Ted, I'm sorry. Indeed, it's always one thing or another. And now the situation has forced me to stay in Scotland a bit longer. But I think next year I'll definitely come to visit you guys."

"We'll be waiting," he said enthusiastically.

"Honey, let me have a better look at you. You've always been a beauty, but it turns out, beauty has no limits. You're radiating in feminine beauty more than ever, and you've lost a bit of weight, too," Arline added.

"Thanks, mom, you also look great."

Arline was truly a very striking woman. Luxurious chestnut hair, thick and always nicely styled. Brown eyes shone with constant joy, and since she met Ted, a smile almost never leaves her face. Slightly taller than her daughter, Arline had preserved her youth very well, and when they walked side by side, they were often taken for sisters.

"Ladies, I think it's time for us to leave the platform. We have plenty of time to discuss all the news and exchange compliments," Ted said with a smile and wheeled the suitcase towards the exit.

The women followed him. Arline put an arm around her daughter's shoulder, "What do you think of the apartment I chose? Did you like it?"

"Yes, it's very nice. Spacious and modern."

"Have you had a chance to walk around or were you resting, waiting for us?"

"I walked the entire Royal Mile and a bit of Princes Street. I adore this city. Naturally, I couldn't just sit still. I dropped off my suitcase, washed my hands, and immediately went out to wander the streets."

"That's so like you! Always on the move. That's why I was so surprised that your stay at Castle Mal dragged on for so long! You could die of boredom there! Despite all your assurances that you were tired of London, I doubt that's true. Two weeks would have been enough to regain your strength."

"We're almost there. We'll talk about this later," Megan evaded a direct answer. "Let's unpack, rest for about half an hour, and then grab a bite to eat. That's when we can share all our news and thoughts."

"As you wish, dear," Arline said, hugging her daughter.

They went up to the rooms on the second floor of the house on Princes Street. In the center of the living room, there was a sofa and a round glass table for four; a kitchen set was against the wall. The doors from the living room led to the bedrooms.

"Megan, you must have already picked a room for yourself. Which one is ours?" asked Ted.

"Choose whichever one you like," the girl responded. "To me, they seem absolutely identical." She took her suitcase and headed to the bedroom after Ted had chosen one for himself and his wife.

"Let's meet for dinner in thirty minutes, okay? Will that give you enough time to freshen up?"

"Absolutely," said Ted, and Arline nodded in agreement.

Megan unpacked her suitcase, hung up all her clothes, arranged her cosmetics in the bathroom, and sat on the edge of the bed, unsure of how else to pass the time. She pondered again whether to tell her mom about Derek or keep it a secret for now. Weighing the pros and cons, she decided it would be better to keep quiet for the time being. Firstly, Arline would be scared that her love-struck daughter might decide to settle down in a godforsaken place, as she considered it. Secondly, Megan found it difficult to describe her relationship with Derek. He sneaks into her room through the window at night and disappears before dawn. They don't go out together, he never calls her... and so on. Megan realistically assessed the situation, hardly anyone would take such a romance seriously. Telling her mom would only worry her to death. The decision was made, she would only talk about her beloved once there was some certainty about his intentions.

"Dear, we're ready," she heard Arline's voice coming from the living room.

"I'm coming! I'm ready too."

Within ten minutes, they entered a Spanish restaurant. Choosing a secluded table in the corner to ensure privacy, and after placing their orders, Arline asked, "Megan, I'm curious to know the details of your relations with your relatives. You said over the phone that all was well but didn't give any details."

"I've become very close with Warren and his wife Glenn. They are about my age."

"I remember Warren as a little boy. Such a sweet kid. Now he's grown up. God, time flies so fast. Keep going, keep going..." Arline said fondly.

"They live in Castle Mal. They moved in with granddad during the last months of his life to take care of him. Then I asked them to stay. I was scared to be in such a big castle alone."

"And Gregor, he doesn't live there anymore?" her mom asked, surprised.

"He does. But you hardly ever see him. He moves like a shadow. Even more frightening. Anyway, with Warren and Glenn, I feel much safer and happier. We see Duncan and Alaric about once a week — usually for family dinners. They're very friendly towards me. Once I return, we're planning to visit them again at Castle Raven. Recently, we all went to the islands where the Ring of Brodgar is. And before that, I attended the fern blooming festival. It was very interesting! Of course, I'm learning about whisky production at the distillery. And the castle's library! You probably remember... Overall, mom, I'm not bored there. I love walking through the heather fields. Either, Glenn and I walk together, picking flowers and talking about everything under the sun, or, I enjoy the freedom, and scents of Scotland alone. You can't get these experiences in London. I'm getting to know the customs, traditions, lifestyle, and I love it all. I think you were too quick to call this place godforsaken."

Arline sighed, "Since it's your first time there, I suppose you would find it interesting. Just don't stay too long. You know Sam needs you in London. Your life is there, Megan."

"I'm in touch with Sam and the bank every day, don't worry."

"But have you decided when you're coming back?" Arline persisted.

"I think in two to three weeks," Megan lied to prevent a persistently difficult conversation with her mother.

"Oh my God! Another three weeks!" Arline exclaimed in dismay.

"Mom! Don't pressure me. Can't I have a vacation wherever I want every few years without limiting myself in time?" Irritation was evident in her voice.

"Sorry, honey, I won't anymore."

"You better tell me, how are things with you? What have you been up to?"

"Everything's calm. A measured lifestyle, as always. We travel a lot. We've already been all over the States and Canada, and we plan to fly to Australia in a couple of months," Arline shared their plans.

"That's so great! You've always dreamed of going there!" Megan was happy for her mother.

"Dreams do come true — thanks to my dear Ted," she looked at her husband with tenderness and love, and he returned her gaze in the same way.

At that moment, Megan thought about how wonderful it would be to travel the world with Derek. To share experiences with each other. Why does everything have to be so complicated? Why can't life be as easy and carefree as her mom's.

"I've been really into tennis and learning Spanish lately," Arline said enthusiastically.

"Why Spanish?" Megan laughed, diverting from her thoughts.

"I've always wanted to start learning a foreign language."

"How's it going?"

"Not very well, yet," her mom admitted sadly.

"Still, you're doing great! You definitely don't lack energy. You can't sit still. We're alike in that way," Megan turned to her stepfather, who had been silent until now.

"Ted, what about you? Tell us."

"Just like your mom," he said with a smile. "Thank God, it's a calm period. Stocks are up and so is our income. When you have both time and money, it's a crime not to travel. Which is mainly what we do. Traveling is our drug."

"Come here more often, I'd love to see you! I miss you a lot," Megan said tenderly.

"My dear, we miss you too; you've got no idea how much," Arline said with bitterness. "I can't forgive myself for leaving you alone. I should have insisted you come with us to the States."

"Don't blame yourself. Everything's fine, and I wouldn't have gone to America anyway. We would have just ruined our relationship if you had insisted."

"I'm sorry I left you."

"Mom, dear, stop! I'm very glad you're happy. Now I understand that you had a valid reason to move. You see, everything's good with me. I've graduated from university. The restaurant business is going well. You have nothing to criticize yourself for. That's final."

"Thank you for your understanding," tears of gratitude shone in her mother's eyes.

*****

They continued talking for a long time, discussing all the latest news about friends, acquaintances, and relatives. They shared impressions of their travels. Megan asked questions tirelessly. Ted and Arline were fascinating storytellers, and she could listen to them for hours on end.

When they entered the apartment, Ted left them alone in the living room, saying he wanted to go to bed early, and that the two of them might have secrets best not heard by men. Megan mentally thanked him for this — she really was waiting for a chance to be alone with her mom, to finally ask her the question that was troubling her.

They sat down at the table with cups of English tea and Megan's favorite biscuits.

"Mom, please tell me the truth, why did you move to London? And what did grandfather never forgive you for, even before his death?"

Arline sighed heavily. She didn't want to sift through painful memories and stir up the past. But she knew that if her daughter had asked this question, she wouldn't give up until she heard an answer. That was her character.

Arline still tried to avoid the conversation.

"It's such an old story, it doesn't matter anymore."

"For me, it's important. Please, tell me. I have the right to know what happened in my family. What's the real reason for your quarrel with grandfather? All I know is that you and my father separated before I was born. You had a fight with grandpa and moved to London, where you gave birth to me. But obviously, there's more to it than that."

"Alright, then listen from the beginning to the end, and please, don't interrupt me."

Megan nodded, and Arline began her story, "To me, the North of Scotland always seemed wild and barbaric. It's as if it got stuck in the Middle Ages. Your grandfather had a best friend, an Irishman named William O'Connor. The O'Connor family had a significant influence in Ireland. Like our clan, they were involved in whiskey production. In the North of Scotland, they acquired a shipping company. My father and William had been planning for years about my union with William's son, Marcos. Marcos was a year older than me and, in your grandfather's opinion, was an excellent match. The fathers had everything planned in advance and were waiting for the right time to formally announce this idea. This marriage would have united two solid clans and strengthened the family business, making it more promising. It would have ensured economic stability for the McKenzies for many decades to come. I think you can understand that those ideas were not to my liking. I never loved Marcos and wanted nothing to do with him. He was a proud, arrogant man with despotic tendencies. I understood that he was the type of man who, if something displeased him, could raise a hand against a woman. But my father wouldn't listen to anything. My objections to the marriage were ignored. I was a young girl, dreaming of true love and the joys of life, brimming with energy. I dreamt of moving to a big city, attending university, and making friends. Attempts to talk to my parents about the modern world, the right to choose, human freedom, and so on, were futile. If my father set something in his mind, no one could persuade him otherwise. He was a very difficult person. My wedding with Marcos was set to take place on the second of August, on my nineteenth birthday. My mother informed me about this in the beginning of May. Hearing this news, I cried and ran to the sea. Sitting on the shore, lost in thought, I didn't notice a young man approaching me. Handsome, cheerful, and energetic, he handed me a handkerchief and mentioned he was passing through, staying at a hotel near Castle Mal. He tried his best to cheer me up, which he easily did. He was twenty-six and came from London. His name was Richard. That's all I knew about him, and at that moment, it was all I needed. It was love at first sight. We had a whirlwind romance. He came from a well-off family and could afford to extend his stay at the hotel for as long as he wanted, which he did. After two months of our secret meetings, my mother found out – she followed me one day. Something in my behavior seemed odd to her, and she decided to clarify everything. Naturally, upon learning about my relationship with Richard, she told my father. He threw a terrible scandal, hit me in the face, and locked me in my room. For two weeks, I couldn't go outside, and thus, couldn't inform Richard about what had happened. A maid, who was working for us at the time, secretly told me that a young man had come, wishing to see me. But he was met by Malcolm, and they talked in the office for about half an hour. Then the young man left. Walked away from my life forever. When I was finally allowed to leave my room, I immediately went to the hotel where Richard was staying. There, I was told that he had left three days ago. I was distraught with grief. My wedding day with Marcos was approaching, and my desperation grew with each passing day. Back then, there were no mobile phones. I didn't know Richard's address, didn't know how to find him. What your granddad told him remains a secret to this day. A few days before the wedding, I realized I was pregnant. I didn't know what to do, and decided to confide in my mother, hoping the marriage would be canceled. Unfortunately, my mother was entirely on my father's side, she supported him in everything and, just like him, had high hopes for my union to William O'Connor's son. She categorically stated that there was only one way out – to get rid of the child; the wedding had to proceed. That day, we had a huge argument, I ran out of the house and rushed to the sea. I didn't know what to do or how to be. There, on the shore, a man approached me, looking to be in his thirties, and he seemed to radiate peace and tranquility. He started asking what happened and why I was crying so bitterly. He wondered if he could help in any way. At that moment, I desperately needed someone to share my experiences with. I needed advice on how to move forward. After listening carefully to my story, he said that under no circumstances should I end my child's life, that I needed to run away from Castle Mal as soon as possible, and try to find Richard. I replied that I had thought about this, but I didn't have the funds for even a ticket to London, let alone rent a place and provide for myself. My whole life, my parents had always fully supported me, bought everything necessary; I never had any financial responsibilities up until that point. Daniel, which was the man's name, said that my main task was to hold on for twenty-four hours until the next evening, and not let my parents take me to the hospital. Meanwhile, he would gather the necessary amount for my move to England. It was hard to believe that a stranger was willing to selflessly help a girl he had met for the first time in his life. But it was my only hope, and I trusted him. We made an escape plan. Daniel talked through all the details, after which I went home. It was already late, around midnight. When I returned to the castle, my father was furious. He said that my mother had had a heart attack because of me, and if something happened to her, he would never forgive me or would kill me with his own hands. My mother had heart problems since childhood, and the stress she experienced due to my pregnancy severely affected her well-being. I entered my mother's room to talk to her calmly, but she didn't want to listen, she said that only my termination of the unwanted child and marriage to Marcos, could save her."

Arline delved into the heavy memories of her last conversation with her mother. Then she spoke again, and Megan could almost see everything happening on a screen, "You, ungrateful wretch, Arline! You have dishonored our family. I would have thrown you out of the house like a stray dog, if not for our arrangement with O'Connor! Your father and I had high hopes for you, and you betrayed us. Not only did you spit in our faces by getting involved with a transient Englishman, but you also got pregnant by him! I devoted my life to raising you. You were supposed to become a true lady, a real McKenzie! Instead, you became a shameful harlot, bringing disgrace upon our family. Get out of my room this instant! I do not wish to see you anymore."

"Mom, I love him, do you understand? I don't want to marry without love," cried Arline.

"I repeat: get out of my room. Tomorrow, your father will solve all the problems, and you will marry Marcos, whether you like it or not."

In tears, Arline, headed to her room.

That night, Arline's mother had another heart attack... and died. Malcolm, beside himself with grief and anger, burst into his daughter's room, hit her in the face again, and in his fury, called her a murderer, blaming her for the death of her mother, whose heart wasn't able to bear the shame that her daughter had brought upon the family. Mother would not have left this world so young if not for Arline, whose actions drove a forty-six-year-old woman to her grave.

"I had no choice but to wait for the agreed time and run away," she continued, "Daniel, as he promised, approached the castle at 1 a.m. I managed to make a rope out of sheets, and descended from the window into the courtyard. I took only a small bag with me. Daniel knew the shortcut to Thurso well. We walked through the hills for about three hours; I was very tired and often stopped. In the town itself, we waited for the first train's departure near the station, not getting too close. I feared that my father would have noticed my absence and headed to search at the railway station. Around 4 a.m., Daniel left me, wishing me luck. He handed me a ticket and an envelope with a significant amount of money. I didn't know how to thank him. I asked for his address to repay the debt at the first opportunity, but he didn't leave his contact information. Thankfully, my absence wasn't immediately noticed at home. I boarded the first train departing at 6 a.m.

— and my new and adult life began. Arriving in London, I rented a small room in Hammersmith and got a job as a waitress in the nearest restaurant. All my attempts to find Richard were in vain. I didn't have his address; I didn't even know his last name. Then you were born. My life found its purpose. For the first time in many months of suffering, I found happiness. I took any work that I could find to do from home. I needed to earn money so we could survive. We had very tough times until I was able to send you to nursery. For many years, I couldn't forgive my parents, who ruined my life and deprived you of a father. But everything changed when I met Ted. Now, I don't hold a grudge against anyone, and I'm pleased that things turned out this way. I have you and Ted; I don't need anything more. That's enough to feel happy. I will always remember Daniel and be grateful to him for everything he did for us. If it weren't for him, who knows where we would be now. He was just a stranger who showed true mercy and generosity. He saved your life and mine, girl. May God bless him with happiness and health. Every time I go to church, I pray and thank God for sending him to me when he did."

"Mama! My God! Why have you never told me about this? This isn't just a story; it's a drama of human life!" Megan was deeply shaken by Arline's revelation.

"I saw the warm relationship you were developing with your grandfather over the years, and I didn't want to ruin it. Two years after your birth, our family lawyer contacted me."

"Mr. Douglas?"

"That's him. He inquired about how I was doing, whether I had given birth to the child, and said that Malcolm wanted to communicate with his grandchild. He asked me to arrange a time and place for a meeting. Naturally, I refused, fearing he might harm you. He didn't want your birth, so the worst thoughts were in my head. Douglas periodically called with the same request. By your fifth birthday, I finally agreed to the meetings, but with the mandatory presence of a third person. My father didn't want to see me, so Douglas was present at the meetings for the first year. Then, seeing that your relationship was blossoming, and that grandfather was really becaming quite attached to you, I allowed your meetings to be alone. But I still don't understand why, two years after I left, he decided to get to know you again. What happened in his inner world, that without forgiving me, he decided to communicate with the child who provoked the upheaval of our lives?"

"How much you've had to endure! How strong and brave you turned out to be! To leave home, go to the big city, start everything from scratch. And you were so young. It's a very sorrowful story."

"I believe in fate, Megan. I think it led me in a certain direction and gave me strength to cope with hardships."

"You're a fatalist."

"And you're not?" asked Arline.

"I don't know anymore. Perhaps."

"Nothing happens by chance, my dear. We always end up where we are supposed to be, at the time we are meant to be there. No meeting in this life is by accident. There's always a reason for everything. Either we are missionaries in someone's life, or someone comes into ours with a specific purpose."

"You're right," Megan said.

She felt very sorry for her mother. A serious tragedy played out so many years ago at Castle Mal. Years of Arline's life passing in pain and suffering.

"My dear, I don't want this story to overshadow your fond memories of your grandfather. I know how much you loved and respected him."

"It won't, don't worry. My relationship with him is completely different. He treated me well and was a wonderful grandfather. I know he genuinely loved me and was proud of me," Megan sighed.

"I'll ask you not to try and find your father. Don't stir up the past. I have a happy life with Ted. He likely has a family too. That brief romance is long forgotten. The appearance of an unknown adult daughter could bring discord to his family and cause suffering to his wife and children. The past needs to stay in the past."

"I understand and completely agree with you. If we haven't met by now, then that's how it's meant to be. You are right about missions. He was just a missionary in our life. Having fulfilled what fate had written, he left forever," Megan said with a sad smile.

"You're a very wise girl. My Megan! I'm so glad you understand everything."

"What happened to Warren and Duncan's parents? I feel somewhat awkward asking them this question. I don't want to bring up a painful topic for them."

"After I left, I think all the surrounding areas were only talking about the evil fate that befell the McKenzie family. Six months before the events I told you about, Warren and

Duncan's parents died in a car accident. They were returning from Inverness, and their car flipped on the road. The children were left in the care of their grandfather and his wife. They were still very young. Warren was about two years old, and Duncan was only a few months."

"Did Alaric's son or daughter die?" Megan asked, feeling deep sympathy for the entire McKenzie family.

"His son. That year, my uncle lost his only child, and my father lost his wife and only daughter. What happened to Alaric's wife, I don't know. If you haven't seen her, she has probably already passed away. They were of quite an advanced age."

"Indeed, a cruel fate, so many tragedies happening in one year. It's really sad for everyone," the girl shook her head.

"It's not worth dwelling and analyzing this too much. It won't do any good. Follow my advice and let this story go. You know it now, but there's no need to keep thinking about it," her mother said.

"Okay, you're right. It's late, almost two in the morning. Let's go to bed."

"Yes, let's."

"How are you feeling?" Megan asked, worried that delving into the past might have deeply upset her mother.

"I've moved past it a long time ago and don't feel the pain of those memories anymore, so I'm okay, don't worry about me," Arline replied with a sad smile.

"I hope oo. Goodnight, Mom."

"Goodnight, honey."

This story made a profound impression on Megan. She pondered over the information she had received for almost the entire night. She was very curious about where Daniel, the man to whom she owed her life, might be. Before falling asleep, she decided that upon returning to Castle Mal, she would definitely ask Derek to help find him, so she could express gratitude for the support he had provided her mother.

13

The Secret

The days spent in Edinburgh flew by unnoticed. Megan enjoyed every minute spent with her beloved and cherished family. The story told by her mother elicited even more respect and admiration Megan had towards her. Such a seemingly small and fragile woman proved to be a strong individual, overcoming numerous obstacles on her way to happiness and independence. After that night of revelations, neither mother nor daughter revisited the topic. During the remaining days in Scotland's capital, they walked around a lot. Together, they climbed Arthur's Seat, wandered most of the streets of the historic center, and visited numerous shops and restaurants. When it was time to say goodbye, they cried. It was hard for them to part again.

"Megan, please come to visit us soon. This meeting wasn't enough. We spent so little time together," Arline said, wiping away tears.

"You guys should come over too. I won't be able to visit you until next summer. Maybe you can come to London for Christmas?"

"We'll do our best. I love you, honey," Arline hugged her daughter tightly.

"I love you too."

They stood on the platform waiting for two trains going in opposite directions: one to Thurso, the other to London. After a warm farewell to her mother and stepfather, Megan boarded the carriage and started to replay the events of the past five days in her mind. There was sadness in her heart, but at the same time, she felt warmed by the thought of meeting Derek soon, for whom she had missed terribly. This trip made her realize that she couldn't be without him for more than a few days. She couldn't imagine her life without her beloved anymore...without his cheerful, sometimes mysterious smile, warm hugs and passionate kisses, his stories, and interesting judgments. In just three months, he had become an integral part of her life. She counted the hours until she could see him again. Love is a terrible addiction, one from which there is no strength to escape. Nor is there any need to escape it if it's mutual.

The train arrived at Thurso station at 4:35 p.m. Warren and his wife came to meet their relative. Scanning the small station, Megan thought about how her mother, all those years ago, had fled to London from this very station, never to return. And now, love had brought her daughter back here. What contrasting stories. She marveled at fate, which weaved such strange patterns of reality.

"Megan, Megan!" called Glenn.

Megan joyfully hugged her relatives and said, "I'm so happy to see you again! I've missed you!"

"We missed you too! Tell us, how was your trip to Edinburgh?" Glenn asked eagerly.

"It was great. I'm so happy I got to see my mom. But time flew by so quickly; it felt like we were there for not five days, but a day."

"It's a pity they didn't want to come here."

Megan left this remark without further comment, now fully understanding why her mother avoids this place.

"I told granddad and Duncan that you need to rest today. They already wanted to have a family dinner tonight, but I convinced them to postpone it until tomorrow," Warren joined in the conversation.

"Thank you. Seven hours on the road really takes its toll. I'll just stick to unpacking my suitcase today. And tomorrow, after I've rested up, I'll gladly join you all for dinner," Megan said with a grateful smile, looking at her cousin.

"Excellent. How was the weather in Edinburgh? I assume warmer than here?" he inquired.

"Yes, the weather was good. About six degrees warmer than Thurso, and it's almost winter here, nearing the end of September," Megan laughed.

"That's definitely not winter," Warren said cheerfully, "that's normal weather; slightly autumnal."

"Autumnal, you say…such strong and icy wind. Brr… freezing cold," she said, tightening her light scarf around her neck.

"What did you expect?! It's the north, my dear cousin! It's always like this here. Summer is very short; we get a couple warm months a year. The rainiest period will start soon," Warren said as he loaded her suitcase into the car.

"Alright, I'll survive somehow. How's everything at the distillery?"

"As usual. Nothing worth mentioning."

"No news is good news," she commented.

"Exactly!" Warren agreed.

*****

Entering her bedroom, Megan found the window open, and a black raven perched on the windowsill. Luckily it hadn't flown inside. The window, she figured, had probably been left open to air out the room, or perhaps Derek had been here during her absence. Just as Megan took a step towards the bird, she caught sight of a bouquet of flowers on the bed. There was no doubt – her beloved highlander had been here. He had brought the flowers for her arrival. With a happy smile, she pressed the fragile affirmation of his feelings towards her. This was the first gift from her lover.

I wish he would come soon, she thought, and turning around, saw the raven watching her attentively.

"Beautiful, aren't they? You didn't bring them by any chance, did you?" Megan joked. "Alright, off you go now! I don't have anything to feed you today, sorry. I'll bring you some cookies tomorrow, my little bodyguard."

She carefully closed the window to avoid scaring the bird with a sudden movement. The raven flapped its wings and flew away. After unpacking, Megan took a shower, changed her clothes and went down to the kitchen. During dinner, the girl shared her impressions of the trip and her beloved city with Warren and Glenn. Gradually, the topic of conversation shifted from one subject to another. Having missed each other, the young people couldn't stop talking, eagerly discussing everything. Megan felt slight euphoria at the thought of having such wonderful relatives. How great it was that they appeared in her life! Her mood was excellent, her eyes sparkled with joy and happiness. She was overwhelmed with love and harmony, not having felt so many positive emotions simultaneously for a long time. But even while immensely enjoying the reunion, she kept an eye on the time, remembering that Derek would soon arrive. Seizing the nearest pause in the conversation, she excused herself to her relatives, citing tiredness, and hurried to her room, skipping up the stairs two at a time.

Derek was standing by the fireplace, looking at his watch when she entered the bedroom. He turned around, and his face lit up with a handsome smile. Megan rushed to her beloved. He hugged her tightly and spun her around the room. Their joy at seeing each other knew no bounds.

"I missed you so much!" the girl showered his cheeks, eyes, and lips with kisses.

"For such tender expressions of affection, I'm willing to let you go on trips occasionally," Derek laughed. "But only for a short while. I've missed you terribly and I'm so happy you're back."

"I love you. Thank you for the flowers."

"I love you too. Glad you liked the surprise. How was your time in Edinburgh? How was your meeting with your mom?"

"Everything was wonderful! Mom told me a story about her past that made me sad," freeing herself from his embrace, the girl said.

"What story? Or is it a secret?"

"It's not that it's a secret, but I can't say I'm ready to share it with many."

"Am I not on the list of people you trust?"

"On the contrary, you're the only one I can tell this to, no one else."

And Megan described everything that happened to Arline all those years ago at Castle Mal.

He listened attentively to her, not interrupting, and when she finished her story, he said, "I'm grateful to Daniel for saving your life. If that hadn't happened, Malcolm would have sent his daughter for an abortion, and you wouldn't have been born. I can't imagine my life without you now. So, Daniel saved both our lives," he concluded with a smile.

"My mom believes he was from Thurso. Do you know anyone by that name, around sixty years old or so? I'd really like to meet him and thank him on my mom's behalf and my own."

"No, I don't know anyone like that. You're not holding any grudges against your grandfather for what he did, are you?"

"Absolutely not. I think when he met me, he must have blamed himself many times for pushing his daughter in that direction. Grandfather adored me. And this story, as sad as it may be, won't change my feelings for him," Megan's eyes shone with love during this short speech.

"You're a wonderful person," Derek said tenderly, running his finger along her cheek.

"Thanks, you are too," she smiled.

"Can you somehow make inquiries about any Daniels living in Thurso? Of that age? You work in administration, there must be something you can grasp onto."

"I'll see what I can do tomorrow. I'll try my best to find him."

"Thank you," she said again, kissing her beloved in gratitude.

For a while longer, Megan recalled specific moments from her trip to Edinburgh. It turned out that Derek also loved the city and would like to move there. Then, after a romantic night and passionate declarations of love for each other, he left her room at dawn, as always. She didn't hear him leave, as she was sound asleep in his arms, exhausted after the long journey.

The next day she was simply on cloud nine with love. During the day, she and Glenn went shopping in Thurso, and stopping by a famous French patisserie, they bought a beautiful cake for the family dinner; a two-tiered masterpiece of culinary art made of layers of sponge cake soaked in aromatic liqueur. The cake was covered in glossy, shiny chocolate glaze, adorned with exquisitely beautiful flowers made of marzipan and cream. Megan was eager to delight Alaric and Duncan with this magnificent dessert; both had a sweet tooth.

While having lunch in a restaurant, Glenn saw an acquaintance who happily joined their table, and jumping from one topic to another, started talking non-stop. At first, Megan was amused, but then she began to feel sorry for the girl. Perhaps the reason for such talkativeness lay in the lack of social interaction and events in the small town. The thought visited her that it was time to leave soon, or she too would eventually have nothing left to say. She would be just as likely to spout nonsense, just to avoid silence. The day passed quickly, and when they returned to the castle, it was time to get dressed and go to dinner at Castle Raven.

*****

"Alaric, Duncan, I'm happy to see you! How are you?" Megan said, kissing them in greeting.

"We're also glad to see you, girl," the head of the family smiled in response.

"How was your trip?" Duncan asked.

"Great! Look what Glenn and I bought for dessert today," she handed over a box with a transparent top through which one could see the masterpiece by a French chef.

"What a marvel!" Alaric appreciated.

"I think we'll start dinner with the dessert," Duncan joked, taking the offering from Megan's hands.

Everyone laughed and proceeded to the dining room, where the table was set. Starting the meal, the clan head of the McKenzies, for the first time during their acquaintance, inquired about Arline's life, "How is your mother doing?"

"Mom's fine. She's returning to the States with Ted tomorrow."

"Is she happy in her marriage?"

"Very."

"Glad to hear it."

They did not speak further about Megan's mother.

"Duncan, how's work going?" the girl inquired, aiming to keep the conversation going.

"All good. We had some troubles with our English partners last week, but we've already sorted everything out," he shifted topics and continued, "Warren tells me you really liked our library and you're ready to move in with us right after you finish all the books at Castle Mal. I hope this will be sometime soon? Or have you got your suitcase with you today already? We'd be delighted," Duncan said with a playful smile.

"We did some rough calculations: turns out, it won't be that soon," Warren responded cheerfully.

"She'll have to spend a few more years in Castle Mal's library to read all the books. So, brother, she stays with us for now, much to our delight."

"Pity. Well then, just make sure you visit more often," Duncan said, raising his glass to his cousin.

"I promise, I will! If I may, with your permission, I'd like to take you up on your offer to access the library in about fifteen minutes. I'm looking for a particular volume I couldn't find at Castle Mal. While you enjoy your whiskey by the fireplace, I'll explore your printed treasures."

"Of course, Megan. You don't need to ask for permission in this house; you may go wherever you like," Alaric stated.

"Feel free to take all our books if you like; we won't mind," Duncan winked at her.

"When Megan says, 'I'll just pop into the library for a bit,' it means she'll be there for at least three hours," Warren commented.

"I know I could get lost in there for days, but don't worry, Warren. I won't overstay my welcome with my dear relatives.

By the time your glasses are empty, I'll be back. And if I somehow lose track of time, please call out to me before you leave."

"You're welcome to stay the night here; we'd be happy to have you," Alaric offered.

"Grandpa's right, stay over! We can make up a bed for you in the library, or even better, in Margaret's room," Duncan teased her.

"Stop making fun of me," Megan laughed.

"You always have such a serious look on your face, love; I just have to cheer you up every time."

"Thanks for your kindness! I'll go now before you start teasing me again."

"Aren't you going to finish your cake?" he asked, raising his eyebrows in surprise.

"I've already had one piece; that's enough for me. No need to overindulge in sweets."

"Ah, you have rules and limits for everything. Such a perfectionist! Then I'll finish your piece too. It's insanely delicious!" Duncan said, dragging her plate towards himself.

"Enjoy it!"

Megan was glad to find an excuse to avoid drinking whiskey by the fireplace. Firstly, she wasn't a big fan of this type of alcohol. Secondly, she quickly got tired of monotonous conversations that lasted for two hours. She felt that dining with relatives was more than enough social interaction for her.

Once in the library, the girl began inspecting the books starting from the lowest shelves. Her gaze moved higher and higher across the rows of ancient volumes. However, the book she was looking for remained elusive. Megan used a small library ladder, and standing on its second rung, continued her search. Meanwhile, she absentmindedly twirled a thin ring on her finger, taking it off and putting it back on. At one moment, the ring slipped from her hand, rolled across the floor, and disappeared behind a cupboard. Cursing her clumsiness, she descended the ladder and pondered her next steps. She then remembered that this cupboard was actually a door to a storeroom where all sorts of junk were kept, as Duncan had explained during a tour of the castle. Carefully entering the abandoned space, she turned on the light and realized there was nothing frightening inside. Indeed, the area was cluttered with junk: antique furniture that was surely over a hundred years old, odd boxes, paintings, and a plethora of other items. The girl knelt down and began searching the floor for the tiny object. The light was dim, requiring great focus to find such a small item.

Soon, Megan began to shiver from the cold; there was a window slightly ajar in the upper right corner of the storeroom. She decided to close it, but upon getting closer, realized she couldn't reach the sashes. Looking around, she noticed a row of paintings along the wall, covered with sheets. She chose a smaller canvas to help her close the window. However, the discovery piqued her interest. They turned out to be portraits: men and women from the Drummond clan. After looking at a few, she was about to resume her interrupted search, but then froze. One of the portraits caught her attention. At first, Megan looked at the image in bewilderment: from the half-meter dusty canvas, the handsome face of Derek looked back at her. A black and white checkered plaid, like the one he occasionally wore, was draped over his left shoulder. And on the frame at the bottom, a golden plaque bearing an inscription:

LORD DEREK DRUMMOND 1896

Megan's legs buckled, a chill ran through her, and in a state of shock, enveloped her entire being. She pressed her palms to her cheeks. In a fraction of a second, a memory of one of the meetings with her beloved, flashed through her mind. That night, getting up, Megan threw back the blanket from the bed. The kilt, which Derek had carelessly thrown over the blanket, slid to the floor. Picking it up, the girl felt something cold in her palm. It was a kilt pin, used to fasten the lower part of a man's skirt to prevent it from being blown by the wind. On the clasp, one could see a raven, the crest of the Drummonds. Asking why he had this emblem, she learned that nowadays pins with any heraldry could be bought in souvenir shops or clothing stores. Derek said he didn't attach any significance to it and, if she hadn't asked, he wouldn't have even known there was a bird depicted. Then, his answer completely satisfied her. But now she realized that he had lied to her that night.

Megan couldn't recover. She stood in front of the portrait and quietly said, "Oh my God, this can't be! Such things don't happen! It must be an ancestor of Derek's."

Warren's words came back to her, "The last Lord Drummond left no heirs and had no relatives." Scene by scene, the elements of her nighttime visitor's costume flashed before her mind's eye: the kilt pin with a raven, the kilt, the cloak – identical to the portrait. And his disappearances before sunrise and appearances after sunset...

"It's his great-grandfather," she reassured herself, logically. But in her head, it still echoed, "...Lord Drummond left no heirs and had no relatives... no heirs and had no relatives..."

"No! Please, please, no! I can't... this is impossible..." Megan whispered, becoming more and more aware of the true state of affairs. She started to shake violently from the realization of the nightmare she found herself in, the terrifying reality she was facing. Feeling weak in her legs, the girl sat down on the floor, leaning her back against a large box, not taking her eyes off the portrait. Derek Drummond. Lord Derek Drummond. She read this inscription for the tenth time, as if hoping to find some kind of mistake. Her entire body was seized by an ice-cold terror. Megan could no longer think or move. She could only breathe, but even that was difficult for her. Behind her, there was a rustle, then quiet footsteps. Someone was approaching her. She couldn't turn around and risk becoming even more frightened; as she had already reached her limit. How long had she been on the floor? A minute? Ten? She didn't know.

Derek approached the portrait, and after giving it a quick glance, stood next to it, opposite the girl. Fear and agony were reflected in his eyes as well. He wasn't prepared for such a turn of events. He didn't want her to learn the truth so quickly, and especially not in this manner. It never occurred to him that she might end up in this room and stumble upon his image, which he had long forgotten. He thought he had removed all his portraits from the castle decades ago. He saw the state of shock that now possessed every cell of this fragile girl's body and didn't know what to do, how to explain everything, and how to calm her down. Although the latter seemed hardly possible. Megan shifted her gaze to the face of the man standing in front of her, and his soul seemed to turn inside out, she looked at him as though the devil himself had appeared in front of her. She just sat silently, unable to move or utter a word.

"Megan, please say something," Derek said with pain in his voice.

"Are you the missing Lord Drummond?" she asked with a trembling, weakened voice.

"Yes," he quietly replied.

"I slept with a ghost… with the deceased… and on top of everything, I fell in love with him… Jesus…" she covered her face with her hands.

Derek would have smiled at this comment if not for the tragic nature of the situation.

"I'm not a ghost, Megan, and I'm not deceased. I am flesh and blood. I'm alive," he calmly said.

"Are you immortal?"

"No… mortal, it's just a matter of time."

"So how the hell can you explain all this?" The strong shock turned into hysteria. Megan burst out screaming. Tears streamed from her eyes.

At that moment, voices were heard approaching the library doors. Derek quickly covered the portraits with a sheet, helped Megan to her feet, and forcefully pushed her out the door, into the library hall. But no one entered. Apparently, someone had walked into Duncan's office, which was nearby. As soon as the voices faded, Megan swung the door open again and searched for Derek with her eyes, craving further explanations. The news that her loved one was made of flesh and blood, not a vampire or a deceased, slightly improved her condition. But Derek was nowhere to be found. The girl took a step forward.

"God, he really is a ghost! He disappeared…"

Megan gathered her strength to run away quickly, but before she could take a step, a black raven appeared from behind the door. And then she felt as if she were nailed to the floor. A new wave of horror washed over her from head to toe. Paralyzing fear gripped her soul tightly. In a second, where the raven had just been, black dust and a whirlwind rose up. And then Derek was standing in its place.

Leaning against the nearest wall, the girl slowly slid down it. She couldn't believe her eyes and thought that this might be how people go mad. In a few minutes, her happiness was shattered, and her life turned into a complete nightmare. Transforming from a raven into a human, Derek firmly closed the door. Looking at Megan, one could fear for her sanity. In the girl's eyes, there was no longer fear or pain, they expressed delirium.

"Megan," he said fearfully, taking a step towards her.

"No! No! Don't come near me! Don't touch me!"

She tried to stand up but couldn't. Her body completely stopped obeying her.

"Megan, please, listen…" he implored with a plea in his voice.

"You're a demon! You… you…" she couldn't say another word.

"I am not a demon! I am not dead! I am not a ghost, damn it!" he began to get angry. "I understand that what you've seen in these minutes defies any logic. But there's an explanation for everything. It's ancient witchcraft, performed many decades ago. It's an evil twist of fate. I am chained from dawn till dusk. During this time, I cannot be human; I am a raven. And only when the sun sets behind the horizon can I return to my human form. That's why I always came to you in the evening. Being in the form of a raven, but retaining human logic and perception of reality, I've been able to protect you all day. Especially after the assassination attempt on the day you arrived. And it's unknown to me if the curse of black magic can ever be lifted so that I can return to a normal human life. But I want to believe that one day that time will come, and my torments will end," Derek paused, trying to regain his composure.

Regaining control over his emotions, he continued, "I want you to know: I love you with all my heart and soul. I can't lose you; do you understand? You are the meaning of my life, Megan. I was that Daniel who helped Arline run away to London. I aimed to save your life. I knew even then that you were my destiny. All these years I've been waiting for you..."

"How did you learn this?" she asked quietly.

Gradually, her gaze became more aware, but fear still reflected in it.

"Innes Wallace, the old lady with the heather you once met on the hill, told me. She's a true seer," he replied, secretly glad that she was beginning to respond to his words.

"How did this happen to you? Who cast the curse?" she asked in a lifeless voice.

Derek's eyes reflected deep pain. A sad smile appeared on his face.

"It was an unfortunate accident. How it happened doesn't matter anymore. What matters is how and when this curse can be lifted."

"And how?" she asked quietly.

"I hope you can help me. But I don't yet know how. If we find a way, I can return to a normal life. We can be happy together."

The overwhelmed girl couldn't respond. She wasn't fully aware of what had happened to her in the last hour. The only thing she understood was that she had faced the worst fate imaginable.

"Megan, I beg you, please don't return to London yet. I understand you need time to comprehend the full reality of what is happening. But please, gather your courage, don't run away from me. I'm not happy about my situation either. This is a test for our feelings. We need to get through it. Promise me you won't leave," Derek pleaded desperately.

Megan looked intently at his face. Just an hour ago, it was the most beloved and familiar to her, but now it caused fear and distrust. The person she loved most in the world had subjected her to a real nightmare. She couldn't promise him anything now. She didn't know how to carry on, and whether she would be able to survive this night at all. Would her psyche and reason withstand such a shock? Or would her heart stop, like her grandmother's did, after hearing the news of her daughter's pregnancy? It seemed to her that she would never wake up again as a healthy, contented person.

"I want to go home. I want to be alone. Please, step back, let me go," she said in a dull voice.

"Are you still afraid of me?" Derek asked bitterly.

"I don't know anything anymore…I don't understand. I want to go home…" she said again, covering her face with her hands.

The unhappy lord's soul was torn apart, he felt sorry for his beloved, but at the same time, he was angry. Why didn't she believe him when he had explained everything? And if she got frightened and ran away, then what? Why was she so weak and cowardly? Why couldn't she show more courage?

He tried to help her to her feet. She recoiled from him. All he could hope for now was that she would come to her senses, and they could have a calm discussion. If she truly loves him, as she said, then love should conquer fear. Love can conquer anything if it's mutual. Wobbly, on unsteady legs, Megan made her way towards the hall. Once there, she wondered how much time had passed since she left her relatives?

Gathering all her strength and courage, she entered the castle hall, trying not to reveal her condition.

"We were just about to come looking for you," Warren said upon seeing her.

"Megan, are you alright? You're very pale!" Glenn expressed concern.

"Did something happen?" Duncan asked worriedly.

"I suddenly felt unwell… probably a sharp drop in my blood pressure; it's happened a couple of times before," she mumbled.

Her relatives looked at her with concern. She had gone into the library healthy and happy, in great spirits, her eyes shining with joy. But just an hour later, they saw a pale girl with a disturbed and broken look in her eyes. Assuming she was indeed ill, they ended the conversation, helped her into the car, and took her home. Glenn accompanied her friend to her room and helped her get into bed, extremely worried about Megan's condition.

"Can I do anything else for you?" Glenn asked with care.

"No, thank you. Go to sleep and don't worry about me. I'll be fine," the weakened girl replied.

"Alright, but if you need anything, call me."

Megan nodded.

14
Realization

Megan couldn't sleep all night, but she didn't have the strength to get out of bed either. She kept going over the events of the last few hours in her mind. Sleep only overtook her around seven in the morning, when it was already light outside. At noon she was awakened by a knock at the door and the sound of Glenn's worried voice.

"Megan, are you alright?"

"Come in," she barely managed to open her eyes.

Her head felt so heavy that she doubted she could lift it from the pillow. But then, the memories of the previous evening flooded back, making her feel even worse. For a while, she had hoped it was all just a nightmare. But to her great dismay, she was facing an unearthly reality.

"How are you feeling?" her friend asked, sitting down on the edge of the bed next to her.

"I don't feel well," she whispered lifelessly.

"I'll tell Warren to go fetch a doctor from Thurso."

"Thank you, Glenn, but there's no need. I'll stay in bed for a while, get some rest. I'll feel better tomorrow," Megan tried to convince her.

"Are you sure it's just your blood pressure? At your age, that shouldn't be happening. If it's really that, then you should get it checked out. It could be dangerous."

"Yes, I know. It very rarely happens to me. I'm probably just overwhelmed. The meeting with my mom, the trip, the change in weather, everything together. Don't worry, it will be fine. I promise. I just need a bit more sleep," she said, managing a weak smile.

"Yes, get some sleep, I'll leave you alone. Sleep is the best medicine. I'll check on you later, okay?"

"Okay," Megan replied, grateful for the chance to be alone again.

*****

After spending a whole day alone with her thoughts, Megan managed to overcome the shock. However, she still needed a bit more time to comprehend what had happened and to plan her next steps. Throughout the night, she experienced several stages: first terror, then despair and denial of reality, and by dawn, a sense of hopelessness and acceptance. Now, the emotional tension had been replaced by physical fatigue and a headache. But this allowed her to analyze the situation. By evening, Megan ate everything Glenn brought for dinner, with a ravenous appetite.

She had a nightmare that night: an old abandoned cemetery in London, tombs opening, the dead rising. It was dark, and she was running. Then the scene changed, and she was in Derek's arms in Castle Mal. He was comforting her, and then he walked to the window, turned into a raven, and flew away.

Megan woke up early, but despite the troubling dreams, she felt much better than the day before. The events of the last thirty-six hours needed careful consideration. With a clear and bright mind, it was easier to do so. She finally realized that Derek was a person, not a ghost. And that she still loved him. Despite everything — or contrary to everything — she would be with him. She wouldn't leave him in trouble. Together, they would find a way to return his normal life. Throughout these months, he had never caused her pain or harm. From him, she saw only manifestations of love and care.

He didn't come yesterday, and the raven didn't show up either. He probably thought I would leave him and return to London, she pondered. Her intuition told her that he should appear soon. The main conclusion she arrived at was that true, mutual love is a feeling capable of radically changing a person's thinking and actions. It's the readiness to give up everything and delve into a world of darkness, going through seven circles of hell in the fight for happiness with a loved one. Such a struggle makes sense when love is mutual. Megan was sure of Derek, as she was of herself. This meant that their joint fight against all life's trials would be justified. What happened, happened. Now it was necessary to think about how to fix it.

Getting dressed, Megan remembered her dream in one of the first nights after her arrival at the castle. Margaret and Mary talked about how everything could still be fixed.

For a moment, she froze in place and exclaimed, "Bloody hell! Margaret! She was Derek's fiancée! I didn't connect these parts of the story at all, he loved her! Ugh…" she caught her breath and continued her monologue, lowering her voice to a whisper so no one could hear her, "Calm down, Megan! That was over a hundred years ago. It's all in the past. He has long since stopped loving and has forgotten her. Now he loves only you. It doesn't matter who loved whom before! I also had a fiancé, so what now?! It's better not to think about Margaret at all."

Leaving her room, Megan thought about the difficult conversation with Derek ahead of her. To understand how to help him, she needed to know how and why everything happened. There was no escaping the past. But first, she needed to eat, as she was overwhelmed by a fierce hunger that signaled her physical recovery.

Descending downstairs, she saw Glenn carrying a tray with sandwiches and porridge from the kitchen.

"Is that for me?"

"How are you feeling? I made you breakfast," Glenn said, assessing her friend's condition with a careful look.

"Thank you, you're a true friend!" Megan hugged her by the shoulders and kissed her cheek. "I'm feeling much better, let's have breakfast together."

"Thank God! I was so worried! Come on, you need to eat to gain strength."

Sitting at the table and taking a few sips of strong tea, Megan asked, "Could you tell me where Innes Wallace lives?"

"You want to visit her?" Glenn was surprised.

"I've been tormented by a question from the past for a long time. I was hesitant, but now I think it's time to ask it," Megan lied smoothly.

"If you want, we can go to her right after you finish your porridge and sandwiches."

"Yes, that would be great. If you haven't got anything urgent to do, I'd really appreciate it if you'd take me to her."

"What could possibly be urgent around here! You know I'm always free. So, I'd be happy to go with you. Just make sure you're feeling well."

"Don't worry. I'm perfectly fine. And a walk in the fresh air will only do me good. Glenn, you're simply amazing," smiling at her friend, Megan eagerly anticipated meeting Innes. She believed that the old lady could shed some light on Derek's secret.

Glenn started to excitedly share, "Last year, Paul Ferguson got sick. He was diagnosed with a terrible disease, and it looked like he would need surgery. He went to Innes. She gave him some decoction and recited a charm. The doctors were surprised when the follow-up tests showed nothing. To this day, he's alive, healthy, and feels great. The whole area talks about how she saved him. Can you imagine? She helps everyone, in any situation. I'm sure she can help you too!"

After finishing breakfast, they left the castle and headed straight to the seeress. For about fifteen minutes they walked through the heather field, then along the road for a while until Glenn turned towards a timbered-style house. This building style existed as far back as the Middle Ages. Wooden posts were buried in the ground, rods were hung on them, rafters were laid on top and covered with a straw roof. The walls of the buildings were made of clay mixed with branches, straw and reeds. This mixture filled the space between the frame elements.

Megan expected to see a different type of house. She thought it would be located in the middle of the forest and resemble the home of a witch from a fairy tale. But the dwelling turned out to be quite ordinary, white in color, with brown wooden beams. Approaching the door, Glenn boldly knocked. They waited a couple of minutes, but no one opened. Megan was nervous, fearing that Innes was not home, or that something had happened to her, and she would no longer be able to answer any questions.

The girl wanted to talk to the seeress so badly that she didn't want to delay the conversation even for a few hours. Glenn knocked again. Megan was beginning to lose hope, and they were already thinking of leaving when suddenly footsteps were heard, and the door opened.

Innes took a careful look at the girls and then stopped her gaze on Megan for a few seconds. After a short silence, she said, "I knew you'd come. Come in."

Stepping over the threshold, the friends saw a small cozy hall with furniture from the sixties. Everything was clean and uncluttered. The air was fragrant with various herbs and incense. In one of the glass cabinets, there was a huge array of jars. Each had a label with a name. The labels were made from rolled bandages, and the names were written in pen. In the corner, different medicinal herbs were hung in bunches of ropes to dry.

"Glenn, wait for us here," Innes said before leading Megan along.

The small room adjoining the hall was less bright, with a small window. In the center, there was a round table covered with a crocheted tablecloth. By the window, there was another cabinet, which, like the hall, stored various pouches and jars with powders and tinctures.

"Take a seat, Megan," the old lady kindly offered.

She left the room and returned a minute later with a cup of warm liquid in her hands.

"Drink this, it will help calm your nerves. Your thoughts will become clearer and brighter."

Megan looked at the drink warily. It resembled black tea, but its smell was not very pleasant. Nevertheless, thanking her, she took the cup from the woman's hands and took a sip.

"Don't worry, it's mostly herbs. There are no narcotics in it," the hostess said with a smile.

After drinking almost, the entire decoction, the girl looked up at Innes and asked, "Do you know what happened to me the day before yesterday?"

"If you mean that you found out Derek Drummond's secret, then yes, I know."

"I felt horrified when I discovered the truth, but I think I've managed to overcome my fear because I love him. I want to help him, but I don't know how. Can you advise anything? Is there any hope for salvation? And besides, it's important for me to know how this happened to him," the girl spoke anxiously.

"Hope is always there. You can help him; he has been waiting for you for a long time."

"Do you think he's with me only because he needs help? Is that the only thing that keeps him close?" Megan asked with trepidation, fearing she might hear that the main reason for their relationship isn't love, but an attempt to seek help.

"You shouldn't doubt his feelings. He sincerely loves you. You will find confirmation of my words in time."

"Why hasn't anyone been able to help him for so many years? Do you have any ways to lift the curse? After all, you know a lot and can do much," the girl said hopefully.

"My child, if I could help him, I would have done so long ago. However, the curse placed on him is very strong. It's beyond my power to remove it. I tried, but it was confirmed to me that he could only find release through true love. And the answer to the question of how to save him will be found only by the one destined for him by fate. Therefore, it's you who needs to find the answers, and you who must save him."

"How do I do it? Where should I to start?"

The seer sighed deeply, "A very important event is coming soon, which happens once every four years – the night from November 11th to 12th. You're lucky it's almost a month away. You must not miss this moment, otherwise, you'll have to wait several more years. At midnight, you need to be in the center of the Ring of Brodgar. Sprinkle the altar with a drop of your blood, then lie down on it. Ask a question, and you will be given an answer."

"Are there no other options?" Megan asked fearfully, not at all pleased with such a prospect.

"None."

Megan closed her eyes and pressed her palm to her forehead. Then, gathering her courage and deciding to think it over later, as there was no time to panic now, she continued asking further questions.

"Who did this to him and why?"

Innes looked at her sadly and replied, "It was a mistake. A cruel fate, nothing more. Derek became the victim of intrigue. A victim of deceitful manipulation. And now there's no point in talking about it. You should not dwell on the past; live in the present and think about the future. Otherwise, there's a risk of getting stuck in the past...losing time and chance."

"I see. So, the first thing to do is to wait for the night from November 11th to 12th, get the answer, and then do as I'm told," Megan said slowly, trying to comprehend everything.

"Absolutely correct."

"Everything is clear. Thank you."

Megan realized she faced another trial: encountering something inexplicable and strange. For her love for him, to save Derek, she had to lie on the altar at midnight and face the mystery. Who would give her the answer and in what form? This scared her the most right now.

"It's a tough trial, but you can pass it. You're underestimating your strength. Your happiness is at stake. Fight for it. Walk through life fearlessly, and you will be rewarded with eternal love. True feelings and courage always prevail. Trials are given only to the strong because the weak are doomed to fail," Innes said.

"But I don't think I'm strong or brave enough. I'm probably one of the weak ones. It seems like a mistake by the universe that this trial fell upon me," Megan said, feeling sorry for herself.

"I've already said you're underestimating yourself. If you were weak, you'd now be sitting in your London flat, locked up tight. But here you are, with me, seeking a solution. I've given you a clue: talk to him and support him in his ordeal. Draw strength from love, for it is the most powerful source in the world. Good luck!"

Megan understood the conversation was over. Innes wouldn't say anything more.

"Thank you!" Megan said, getting up from her chair.

As the friends walked away from the house, Glenn asked eagerly, "Well? What did she say?"

"Oh, not much…" Megan replied distractedly.

"How's that possible? She sees and knows everything!" Glenn was not convinced.

"Well, apparently my question was very banal and not as important as I thought. She said everything would resolve itself and to not worry."

"Are you satisfied with her answer? Or were you hoping to hear something more?"

"I'm quite happy with her response; I feel reassured. I probably attached too much importance to this question," Megan replied to her friend, trying to keep her composure, but her mind was swirling with anxious thoughts.

"Well, that's good! She calmed you down, and that's what matters most! Did you ask her anything about the future?"

"No, I didn't. I'm afraid to go there. What if I hear something I don't like? That would really upset me."

"I meant about love…about family."

"No, I didn't ask."

"You're unbelievable! I wouldn't have been able to resist!"

"I think everything will be fine either way."

"Of course, it will; you deserve the best! I would just be so curious: when? where? with whom?" laughed Glenn.

"Thank you," Megan said with a smile. Although she couldn't share the secret of everything happening in her life with anyone, the sincere joy from having Warren and his wife nearby was a blessing. From them, she felt the love and support she needed so much right now. All the way home, Megan's eyes darted around, but the raven was nowhere to be seen.

15
Beloved Raven

The sun had set beyond the horizon and Megan left the castle, heading towards the sea. The weather was calm but nonetheless cold. Knowing the walk would be long, she dressed warmly. Reaching a stone outcrop at the water's edge, she leaned on it, gazing out over the horizon in anticipation of Derek. It didn't take long for him appear. As darkness fell, Megan caught movement from the corner of her eye. The last member of the Drummond clan was walking along the shore towards her. Only a hundred meters separated them. This time, Derek didn't startle her with his sudden appearance. Megan watched tenderly as the tall, handsome figure, dressed in black, approached her.

My black raven, she thought sadly. His presence no longer frightened her. The fear was only for the future and possible surprises, but now she didn't want to think about that. Derek stopped a couple of meters away from the girl, intentionally maintaining this distance. These days, he tried to keep his distance, allowing her to make her own decision without any pressure from him.

Only this morning had he dared to appear at Castle Mal to find out if she had left for London. Then he saw Megan and Glenn heading towards Innes's house. He realized not all was lost, and she had made her decision. And now it was easy to guess that she didn't just come out for a stroll to the sea. She was waiting for him. But he feared that seeing him up close might scare her again. For a while, they silently looked at each other. Megan felt her heart squeeze from the overflowing love for him. Derek stood opposite her with an impenetrable gaze, his hands in his trouser pockets. She knew he was waiting for her to act.

Approaching him and pausing for a few seconds to look into his face, the girl hugged him tightly. Derek took a deep breath, and responding to her embrace, leaned his cheek against her chestnut hair. They stood in silence, hugging, but during those few minutes, they seemed to have said a lot to each other.

Megan felt his warmth, his scent. At that moment, she understood that with him, she feared nothing. She would follow him to the ends of the earth, go through all the circles of hell if needed. She would fight for her happiness.

"Lord Drummond, I love you," she said, not lifting her head from his chest.

He released the embrace, lifted her chin with his hand, and looking into her eyes, responded, "Megan, I love you too. I was afraid you would leave. You turned out to be as strong and selfless as Arline in the face of danger. I admire you."

"Let's sit down," she suggested, pointing to their favorite boulder where they used to spend hours on end talking about everything.

"Today, I visited Innes. I was looking for answers to my questions."

"Did you find any?" Derek asked calmly.

"Some," she sighed and told him everything she had heard from the old woman.

He listened attentively, with a tense expression on his face. When she finished her story, he asked, "What do you think about it? Are you ready to go to the Brodgar altar at midnight?"

"I am, but only on the condition that you'll be by my side and won't leave me alone for even a second, no matter what. I'm scared! But for us, for your salvation, I will do it," Megan said earnestly, looking straight into his eyes.

"Of course, I'll be with you," Derek said.

And Megan continued, "I'm terrified of that night, but we must cope. I want you to become a normal person again and live like everyone else."

"Together, I've got no doubt — we can deal with anything. Please forgive me for subjecting you to such trials. Considering all your fears in life, you are truly a heroic girl for being ready to go further with me despite everything."

"It turns out that the anticipation is more frightening than the actual confrontation with the object of fear. I used to be afraid of the dark and the night, but now I love them, because it's the only time I can be with you. You are a gift of the night. Just two days ago, I was afraid of you; all the mysticism surrounding you terrified me to death. I realize once again that you're the dearest and most beloved person in the world to me. And I can no longer live without you. Better darkness and mystery with you than a quiet and peaceful life without you. And I don't care whether you turn into a raven or a crocodile, I'll stay by your side as long as I'm sure of your love and devotion."

Derek laughed heartily, "Thanks for the crocodile, I'm genuinely touched."

His laughter was so infectious that they both laughed for a long time, until tears came. It was necessary to relieve the tension and bitterness of the last forty-eight hours.

"Derek, how have you lived all these years? And where?"

"As you already know, Castle Raven passed into your family's possession after my disappearance. I could no longer occupy my chamber in the castle. But there is a tower with a room at the top. For many decades, I used a small window on the outside, through which only a raven could fly. Very rarely did I use the secret staircase from the basement, which a person could easily pass through. That's how I spent thousands of nights until I reached your bedroom a few months ago," with a playful smile, he kissed her firmly.

"Good thing you didn't have to sleep on the streets. But what about this secret staircase? What if someone enters the room and discovers you?"

"Don't worry. More than a hundred years have passed, and no one has been able to do it. Most people avoid secret passages, attics, and cellars," he said.

"What will happen when you return to a normal life? Where and how will you live? Will you want to reclaim the castle?" Megan asked.

"It would be foolish to try to reclaim Castle Raven. Imagine the faces of Alaric and Duncan when I show up and announce that I am that same Lord Drummond who went missing more than a century ago," Derek said with a smile.

"Yeah, that would be funny," Megan laughed.

"To say the least. I think it would be better for us to move to Edinburgh or London. In a big city, nobody cares who you are and where you come from."

The girl's face lit up with joy.

"I mean, you don't want to stay here for long, do you? Am I right?" he clarified.

"Yes. What you just said would be like a dream come true. Can such a day really come!? I would be the happiest person in the world."

"I hope it will be so," he said, but then his face darkened.

"We'll do everything we can to end this nightmare as soon as possible. We just have to wait a little over a month. We'll find out how to lift the curse and do it," Megan tried to sound more confident in her words, seeing his fear of failure.

"The main thing is that it's within our power. It's unknown how and at what cost we will have to pay for this," he sighed.

"Haven't you thought over all these years that there might be another way to remove the spell? Maybe the shamans of Tibet? Or to look elsewhere in the world for the most powerful people who work with dark magic."

"I've been thinking about this forever, endlessly searching for answers. But all in vain. Let's start with the night in November, and if that doesn't work out, we'll think further.

The most important thing is not to miss this night, otherwise, we'll have to wait another four years."

"No, no, not four more years. We will make it this year. By the way, since I've decided to stay here, I need to go to London for just a few days. Sam is doing fine without me, but I owe him a visit, even if it's just for a short while. Otherwise, I'm afraid the staff will get too worried, which isn't good for business."

"Of course. I understand. When do you want to go?"

"Next week, I guess. For five days. If you like, you can come with me. I wouldn't mind having a raven in my apartment during the daytime. I can carry you in a travel bag on the train," she said with a mischievous smile.

"Thanks for not saying a birdcage," he laughed.

"Would you prefer to fly to London? I think by the time you get there, I'll have already returned to Castle Mal."

"Megan, go to London in peace, I'll wait for you here. We'll go there together when I can travel like a normal human being. The trip will do you good. You'll get a break from this nightmare you've stumbled into."

"You're right."

"You're freezing, I can feel you shivering. Let's go, I'll walk you back to the castle."

"Just to the castle?" she asked in surprise.

Derek smiled and kissed the top of her head.

"Wherever you say, my princess."

*****

The days leading up to her trip to England flew by unnoticed. Every day, Megan busily searched the internet for information on black magic, spells, transformations, shamans, but found nothing of value. There was nothing even remotely similar to Derek's case. She could only hope that they would find the answers and help they needed in November. Megan preferred not to think about how this would happen, to avoid unnerving herself with even greater fears ahead of time. She comforted herself with the thought that Derek would always be by her side and would do everything possible to ensure that nothing bad happened. They would surely succeed, and they would find true happiness in the very near future. Day by day, she mentally prepared herself for the most positive outcome.

When she reflected on how much her beloved had suffered over the decades, losing his home, name, and freedom, her heart clenched with pity. But she never brought it up, knowing that he could only accept love from her, and that pity and compassion would deeply offend his dignity. Amidst this whirlwind of feelings and emotions, Megan realized she loved Derek even more deeply. A few days ago, she thought her love couldn't grow stronger, but now, learning his secret and his way of life, her love for him had reached its highest peak, if such a thing exists in the universe. Previously, the mystery and unknown surrounding him prevented her feelings from fully blossoming. Now, despite the complexity of their situation, she knew almost everything about him and became the last Drummond's lover, with whom he could be open, and most importantly, himself.

Every evening, they made joint plans for the future, dreamed of travels, which gave them strength and faith in a positive outcome. Every night, before dawn, Derek still continued to leave quietly while Megan slept. He didn't want to shock her with his transformations. In his raven form, he tried not to appear before her, staying out of her sight, but he never lost sight of Megan. Derek feared someone might make an attempt on her life again, and that he wouldn't be able to come to her aid in time.

*****

The day before leaving for London, she was having breakfast in the kitchen when Glenn appeared with a bouquet of wildflowers in her hands.

"Good morning, Megan, how did you sleep last night? I hope without nightmares?"

"Good morning, Glenn. Yes, I rested well. Just fell asleep late, insomnia bothered me again. Sit down, let's have breakfast together."

"I ate an hour ago, and then I went to pick flowers. Look, how beautiful they are," Glenn admired the bouquet.

"Indeed," Megan agreed.

"What are your plans for today?"

"Honestly, I don't even know yet. I'll probably walk around the neighborhood."

"Warren and I will go to town. You can join us if you like."

"I'd love to! So far, I haven't seen anything in Thurso except for the train station, pastry shop and the supermarket," Megan happily accepted the offer.

"Wonderful, then I'll show you the town while Warren runs his errands. Afterwards, we'll pick up some groceries and head back. If you'd like, we can also drive along the coast."

"Thank you, Glenn, that's a great idea. I'll go up to my room, grab my purse, and wait for you in the hall."

"I'll tell Warren you're coming with us. He'll be pleased."

*****

Thurso left the impression of being a small, peaceful town, and the day flew by quickly. Megan and Glenn visited everywhere they could. They peeked into a small church and a Gothic cathedral built in the nineteenth century. Their tour of historical sites was enlivened by stories from Glenn, who grew up there. Out of curiosity, the friends investigated a local bookshop, then finally enjoyed the beauty of a solitary white lighthouse on the shore.

"This is probably my favorite spot in town," Glenn shared. "I used to come here often after school or on weekends. It's the most peaceful corner in the world. The enchanting sound of the sea and just a solitary white lighthouse," the young woman looked at it with a warm, but somewhat sad gaze. "How many pleasant evenings we spent here with Warren before we were married…"

"After moving to Castle Mal, do you often manage to visit your favorite lighthouse?"

"Unfortunately, not as often as I would like, but I always make sure to visit this place every time I come to see my mom."

After this little tour, the girls met up with Warren to have lunch together. Scotland is rich in freshwater rivers and lakes. Along with hunting, fishing has historically been considered one of the ways of obtaining food in a country with harsh climate and infertile lands. Therefore, Warren suggested that this time, they make a choice in favor of seafood, to let his cousin from England appreciate the variety of Scottish cuisine. They ordered several dishes made with salmon, prepared in different ways. Everyone was delighted with the tender stewed fish in cream sauce, as well as the grilled dishes with aromatic herbs and spices.

Enjoying the lunch, Megan gave credit to the local professionals, "I've never tasted fish prepared so deliciously before, even in my own restaurant. But we do have some of the best chefs in London!"

"It's not just the chefs' skill, but also the fact that this salmon grew up in the purest lake and was caught just this morning," Warren noted.

"Thank you for a wonderful day and for the world of Scottish cuisine."

"You don't have to thank us, Meg. We're trying to show you why we love this place so much and why our ancestors lived here their whole lives," said the cousin.

The rest of the day, the small group spent driving along the coastline of the northern part of Scotland.

16

London

The day of departure arrived. Megan boarded the train to Inverness, from where she would continue her journey by plane to London. She left Thurso with positive thoughts and great hopes for the future. She was firmly convinced that she would do everything possible to free Derek from the curse, so they could settle down in the capital of England, but whenever possible, visit the place where Derek was born, grew up, and spent his entire life.

Undoubtedly, the north of Scotland had become very dear to Megan; it had given her love and a wonderful life companion, but she did not want to stay there for good. The monotonous days and ceaseless boredom isn't a life for her. Although, the last two weeks have been eventful with the trip to Edinburgh, Derek's secret, the visit to Innes Wallace...and now, once again, she was on the road.

After several months of absence from London, Megan entered her cozy, cherished apartment. After the huge castle, it seemed quite small, but just as homey. In June, when she left, she could not even imagine that her trip to Scotland would stretch so long. But now, after a few months, she returned to London a completely different person, with different values and views on life.

"Hi, I'm back, but not for long," Megan said greeting her teddy bear, who was waiting patiently in the same spot she had left him. "And if everything turns out as I hope, next time I won't come back alone," she said smiling.

Tired after the long journey, the girl unpacked her suitcase, took a hot shower, and went straight to bed. She planned to spend the next day working at the restaurant.

That night, she slept soundly and without dreams.

*****

"Hi, Sam!" greeted Megan.

He turned around from the cash register with a smile.

"Megan! Great to see you again! I must say, you look wonderful! The vacation in Scotland did you good."

"Thank you!"

Megan had never met anyone as positive as her assistant. For as long as she remembered him, he was always in a great mood. Over the years, Sam had been a faithful and worthy manager of the restaurant. During her absence, she had repeatedly thanked fate for such an employee, on whom she could calmly leave her mother's legacy and go away for so long. Sam was forty-two years old and was a true workaholic, not burdened by family.

"Have you finished all your business in Scotland? Do you no longer need to go back there?"

"I've practically settled all the issues. My cousin manages the factory and looks after the castle, living in it. But I have one small matter left which I think will be resolved by the end of November. After that, I'll finally return to London."

"By the end of November?" he asked, genuinely intrigued.

"Yes, I came back for just five days. Then I have to go back to Thurso," she said with a guilty smile.

"Something tells me there's a man involved here," he said with a smirk.

Megan didn't comment on his remark, so he continued, "I'm managing fine, don't worry. Take care of your business. We're doing well resolving issues over the phone. There are no problems. Your absence doesn't affect the restaurant. It's just important for me that you come back before Christmas, because if you remember, we had agreed on my three-week holiday in advance. You know I would never usually leave the restaurant at this time, but the situation with my father is complicated. I'm afraid this might be his last Christmas, so I need to be with him in America."

"Yes, of course! There's no question about it. I'll be back by the end of November. But if there are any complications, I'll come before the holidays under any circumstances to cover for you."

"Thank you for understanding."

"You've got nothing to thank me for. Let's go to the office and look at the financial reports."

*****

Megan spent all day, from morning to evening, at her workplace. She realized that the staff were perfectly capable at handling their duties and her presence was not necessary, but she couldn't help it. Only once did she leave the restaurant around five o'clock to meet her school friends. Before her trip to Scotland, they used to gather a couple of times a month in famous London pubs to share the latest gossip and discuss events happening in each other's lives. And now everyone was very curious to find out what caused their friend's long absence. Entering the pub, Megan saw Elizabeth, a tall slim blonde, waving at her, inviting her to a table where the six of them were already seated.

"Megan, dear, where have you been?" Peter asked, kissing her cheek.

She had known him since elementary school. A short, dark-haired guy in glasses. He was valued for his intelligence, erudition, and tact. One couldn't ask for a better friend. Peter was always ready to listen attentively, asking no unnecessary questions. He knew how to keep secrets and often provided helpful advice.

"Well, hurry up. Do tell — what's the story with your disappearance," said Doris, hugging her. A pretty girl, not very tall, with a solid build, and was very kind and responsive. If someone was upset, they could always cry on her ample bosom, and she always had words of consolation for everyone.

"We hardly see you as it is, but this time you've broken all records! Did you get a new boyfriend and forget about your old friends?" Melony asked insightfully, hugging her friend. She always knew everything about everyone and could gossip on any topic. Knowing this, friends didn't tell her anything, unless they wanted the whole neighborhood to know about it!

"Megan, what shall we order for you? Ale, as usual?" asked Amanda. This was purely a rhetorical question, as she headed to the bar without waiting for an answer. Amanda was the life of their group, a human firework; a whirlwind in a mini skirt. She couldn't sit still for even a day, always rushing off somewhere unexpectedly. It was she who gathered everyone for picnics, organized performances, invented unimaginable ways to congratulate friends on birthdays and other occasions. And she chose a job that suited her perfectly: organizing parties for children and adults. Today, her hair was dyed bright pink, matching her blouse.

Taking a seat at the table, Megan said with a smile, "Guys, it's great to see you all again! You're totally right; I've kind of dropped out of life for a while."

"Peter told us you've been living in Scotland all this time," said Elizabeth, eager to hear the details of the trip.

"Yes, that's true. My grandfather passed away in June. I went to the north of Scotland to settle the inheritance. It all took much longer than expected, dealing with a whiskey distillery and a castle I inherited. I met with my relatives and familiarized myself with the production technology. A lot of time was spent on financial matters and so on," the girl briefly shared, not wanting to delve into details.

Although she had been friends with everyone at the table for many years, she never shared personal life information with them. Megan considered it a very intimate topic and discussing it with anyone was taboo for her. At the same time, she felt comfortable in the company of friends. She could support any conversation topic, come to the rescue, listen attentively, and give advice if asked.

"A whisky distillery! You're kidding!" exclaimed Peter in surprise.

"No joke, it has belonged to my family for several centuries."

"And what have you done with it?" asked Andrew, who had been silent up until now. Coming from a poor family, he worked in a small office and helped his parents pay for his younger sister's education. He was interested in the financial aspect of the matter.

"We decided that my cousin will manage it. He and his wife will stay in the castle, take care of it, making sure it doesn't fall into disrepair. Maintaining the castle requires significant investments, which will be covered by a portion of the distillery's profits," Megan said, satisfying his curiosity.

"Did you bring us some of your signature whiskey to try?" asked Elizabeth, thrilled by such news.

"Not yet," Megan smiled. "But I'll need to go back there for a couple of weeks to finish up some formalities. I promise, next time I'll bring back the finest Scottish whiskey produced by the McKenzie distillery."

"Make sure you don't forget!" Peter said, raising his index finger.

"I won't. I'm now a major expert on the subject," laughed Megan. "I'll personally select a few bottles of the best drinks for you."

"Wow! Do you really have a castle, like the ones shown in movies?" asked Melony curiously.

"Yes, a big, ancient stone castle. In the first few days, I was even afraid of getting lost inside. One of my rooms is as big as half my London apartment. And it also has very beautiful halls, corridors, huge windows, and a grand library," she lovingly described her new home.

"I read that all castles in Scotland have ghosts. Some are kind and friendly, while others not so much," said Peter with a mischievous twinkle in his eye. "Have you met yours yet?"

"Don't joke like that. Immediately upon my arrival, I asked my relatives about it, and none of them, not even the oldest family member, has ever observed any anomalies," said Megan, thinking that ghosts were the only thing missing from all the mysticism she encountered at Castle Mal. Her psyche couldn't have handled that.

"That's too bad," sighed Amanda. "It would have been fun to have a 'friendly Casper'-style party if Megan had invited us over."

"I'll definitely invite all of you once I settle everything. But don't count on ghosts; we'll find another theme for the party."

She spent the entire evening happily listening to her friends' latest news and actively participated in the discussion of Doris's upcoming bachelorette party. She joyfully shared the news of her imminent wedding, which was set to take place after the Christmas and New Year's holidays, and promised to send out invitations with the exact date and location.

Megan sincerely congratulated her friend, noting that Doris's fiancé was very lucky. Then, the group reminisced about their school and college days. For an hour, they laughed almost to tears without stopping. That evening, Megan felt truly happy. Lately, she had missed such gatherings with friends, the light-heartedness and fun. She went home in a great mood.

*****

The days spent in London flew by in the blink of an eye. On one hand, Megan didn't want to leave her hometown at all, but on the other, she missed Derek terribly and longed to see him again soon. After finishing work on her last evening before departure, she went home. There were still things to pack and preparations to be made for the trip. She planned to go to bed early, as the taxi to the airport was booked for seven in the morning, and upon arrival, a sleepless night awaited her. It was crucial to get a good night's sleep. Before going to bed, Megan talked on the phone with her mom. She knew her daughter had returned home a few days ago and was very happy about the news. However, Megan didn't mention that this visit was only temporary. She deliberately hid the fact that she was returning to Castle Mal the next day. She didn't want to face questions for which there were no answers. And using the vacation and holiday excuse again would be foolish. Her mom wouldn't believe that — she would only get worried, or worse, come to Thurso herself to persuade her daughter to come back home.

After saying goodbye to her mother, she went to bed and joyfully hugged her favorite childhood pillow. She dreamed of returning here soon, but not alone, rather with her beloved. Within minutes, deep sleep overtook her.

She dreamed of a warm summer's day, a bright blooming field near Castle Mal, walking through it, basking in the sun's rays. Ahead, about five meters away, stood a girl with her back to her. She was dressed in a beautiful, expensive blue frock from the late nineteenth century. Her hair was twisted into a bun and hidden under a hat. Megan began to approach her, but the girl ran forward, laughing joyfully and throwing a bouquet of wildflowers over her head, as brides usually do at weddings. Feeling instinctively that she needed to stop the girl and ask her questions, she ran after her, shouting, "Margaret, wait! Please, wait for me!" But the ancestor disappeared. Only the wind brought the answer, "Only I know how to save him, I will reveal the secret to you, find me, and the answers to all your questions will be answered."

When Megan woke up from this dream, it was 5:45. The alarm was set to ring in five minutes. As she washed up and gathered her makeup, she thought about how this must be a sign. Derek's salvation was very close. Perhaps it wasn't necessary to go to the Ring of Brodgar to lift the curse. It was essential to visit the crypt and search Margaret's burial; there surely must be a letter or note she had written before her death.

Such a dream definitely didn't occur without a reason. There is a solution, and it's close by. Megan was eager to share her thoughts with her beloved. Of course, visiting and exploring the burial site was not the most pleasant of activities, rather, it was one of the most terrifying events one could imagine. But if her happiness with Derek was at stake, then it was necessary to grit one's teeth, hold hands tightly, and face destiny. The girl realized that now, with the bright sunlight outside and the crypt still far from her, it was possible to carry on and be brave. The question was whether she could maintain such composure when it came to action, or would she flee at the sight of the tombs and hide under the bedcovers, asking her lover to guard her day and night.

She decided to resort to the most effective method she had been actively using this past month — think calmly as the situation arises, and don't become frightened in advance with unnecessary thoughts, otherwise, nothing will be accomplished. "If I can be the bride of a lord who disappeared over a hundred years ago, and who turns into a black raven, then why can't I visit just one small crypt with Margaret's remains?!" Megan said, encouraging herself out loud. Though inside, everything was turning over from fear.

17

The Crypt

Megan and Warren were approaching Castle Mal. Glancing at her watch, she noted that it was noticeably darker by six in the evening. The daylight had become shorter, which pleased her. She hoped Derek was waiting for her in her room. Upon arrival, citing fatigue after the long journey, she declined dinner and headed to her room. This greatly disappointed Glenn, who was eagerly awaiting her friend to hear the latest news and stories about her trip.

To Megan's surprise, Lord Drummond was not in the room. All the items from the suitcase had already found their place, but he had not come. She tried to compose herself and not give in to anxiety. However, time dragged unbearably slowly, so she went to the kitchen.

"I won't be able to fall asleep on an empty stomach," she explained to Warren and Glenn.

"You've been on the road all day. You need to regain strength with good food and solid sleep," her cousin said.

"You're right, that's the best way."

After chit-chatting with Glenn about the days spent in London and the latest events, Megan went back to her room. This time, Derek did not disappoint her expectations.

"I thought you would come earlier. I waited for you, but then I got hungry and went down to eat."

"Good decision," he said, wrapping his arms around her waist. "I don't think my early arrivals are a good idea. Your relatives will wonder about the reasons for your absence after six in the evening and your regular reluctance to share dinner with them."

"And I'll die of boredom, not knowing how to kill time if you're always going to come late into the night."

"I'll come by at eight. You'll have time to finish your meal by then. Otherwise, I'll feel guilty for making you starve in the evenings."

"Okay then, at half-past seven," Megan bargained. "By that time, we'd be dispersing to our rooms."

Derek laughed, "Agreed, at half-past seven."

"I have something very important to tell you," she began in a conspiratorial tone.

"Go ahead; I'm all ears."

"I had a dream."

"That's good news," he joked, kissing her earlobe.

"Derek, wait, this is serious."

"Of course, my love, go on; I'm listening," he continued smiling.

"In this dream, Margaret said she has answers to my questions and only she knows how to save you. And that I need to find her to uncover the secret."

Derek's expression changed. "How did she tell you this? How did you see her in your dream? Give me more details."

Megan described her dream in detail and added, "I think we need to urgently search her burial in the family crypt."

"Why? What do you expect to find there?"

"There could be some kind of message, like a note she left before she died."

"Megan, what are you imagining? That someone placed a note with her at her request during the burial? That's absurd. You must understand that such a thing couldn't have happened."

"Derek, she said she needs to be found! That means there's something there. We just don't know what it is yet. And to understand, or to find a clue, we need to go there. I think it's logical. It wasn't for no reason that she appeared in my dream."

"You're afraid to enter the crypt during the day with Warren to bring flowers to your grandfather, and now you're planning to investigate Margaret's tomb? It's beyond comprehension!"

"Of course, I won't go alone."

"Are you going to ask Warren to keep you company?" he asked sarcastically.

"Warren has nothing to do with this, I'll go there with you," she calmly replied.

"You know I can't accompany you during the day, and you'll be scared at night."

"We'll go tomorrow after dinner," Megan stated definitively.

"Seriously? You'll run away from there as soon as you step over the church threshold!"

The girl looked at him in surprise, "Derek, I get the impression that it's you who is afraid to go there!"

"I'm afraid for you. I still remember your eyes the night my secret was revealed. I thought you had lost your mind and would never return to your normal state. We must be in the right frame of mind and prepare ourselves for the night in November."

But Megan continued to insist, "Indeed, after that night I haven't been the same. It changed a lot in me. But we need to go to the crypt. Maybe we won't need to wait for the night in November; perhaps we'll find a solution to the problem sooner. In just one day, we might understand how to return you to a normal being, you see?"

Derek looked at her skeptically, not at all thrilled about the prospect of tomorrow evening. He was sure that this idea wouldn't lead to anything useful, and would only cause additional fear for Megan.

"I see you can't be dissuaded. You're like a mule, once you've got something in your head, it can't be knocked out. Tell me, where did you suddenly get such courage to decide to go to the crypt in the evening?"

"I just know that I have to face the nightmare eventually, so it might as well happen sooner. When I was a child and had to get immunization shots, I would go first, even though I was the most afraid. I knew that the quicker I got it done, the less fear there would be in waiting."

"Well, let's take the shot then…" he sighed resignedly, kissing her on the top of her head.

"Tomorrow, at eight in the evening, wait for me at the church entrance. I won't take a single step in there alone. I'm truly terrified, but the thought of you being by my side gives me courage."

Derek looked at his beloved disapprovingly, but nodded in agreement.

*****

The entire next day, Megan tried her best to stay positive and fend off her fears associated with the evening's event. After lunch, they had unexpected visitors, Alaric and Duncan came along with their friend.

"Hello, youngsters! We decided to drop by, sorry for the spontaneity," said the elder McKenzie, kissing Glenn and Megan on the cheek in turn.

"Hello, beauties!" Duncan followed his grandfather's example.

"Fergus! Haven't seen you in ages!" Glenn greeted Duncan's friend with joy.

"I'm glad to see you too!" he replied.

"Megan, meet my school buddy Fergus," Duncan introduced.

"Nice to meet you."

"Likewise, Megan," he politely responded.

In Megan's opinion, the guy was not very appealing. Too pale skinned and watery-eyed with unkempt straw-colored hair that needed a good trimming.

"Wow, such a crowd! How unexpected!" Warren exclaimed joyfully as he descended the stairs to the sound of voices.

"We were just having afternoon tea," Duncan said to his brother and handed Glenn a large box of pastries.

"Darling, could you ask the cook to prepare tea for everyone?" Warren said, wrapping an arm around his wife's waist.

"I'm on it."

"Megan, how was your trip to London?" asked Alaric.

"Great! It was both productive and enjoyable. I plan to return there before Christmas."

"You mean you won't be celebrating Christmas with us?" Duncan asked surprised.

"I need to cover for the restaurant manager; he's going on vacation. And my holiday here has extended quite a bit already."

"Your return to England doesn't mean you won't come to visit us here, does it? We're really hoping for your visits at least a couple of times a year," Alaric said with a warm smile.

"Of course, I'd love to," Megan returned his smile warmly.

"That's wonderful! You know, we're your family and always happy to see you."

"I'm grateful to have found all of you," she sincerely said.

After a pleasant tea in this warm family setting, the girl went to her room, declining dinner. After the delicious pastries, no one in the family felt like eating anymore. In about an hour and a half, Derek would come to discuss the final details of the upcoming plan. Then they would part ways and meet again at the church. Megan dressed in black and tied her hair in a tight bun. In dark clothes, she would remain inconspicuous. As a house-rule, no one sought each other out after dinner. Everyone had the right to privacy and their own personal space. Megan was confident that her absence from the castle would go unnoticed. Such unobtrusiveness by her new family earned Megan's respect and gratitude.

Derek soon appeared. He tried one last time to dissuade his girlfriend from her planned action, but to no avail. He spent some time with her in the room, and ten minutes before the scheduled time, he left for the meeting place.

Megan had previously taken a set of keys to the crypt from her grandfather's desk drawer and now, taking it with her, quietly left the corridor. Having met no one along the way, she left the castle and ran to the church. She was afraid that someone might attack her in the dark, as on her first evening of arrival. The only comforting thought was that Derek was monitoring the situation and would come to her aid if necessary. It was a blessing to have a brave protector.

Reaching the chapel's entrance door, she carefully pushed it open and stepped inside, where only a few electric candles were burning. This lighting was enough to see everything clearly. As they had agreed, Derek was waiting for her there. Gently closing the door, he looked at Megan attentively and asked, "Ready?"

"Yes, let's go," she replied, a bit nervously.

"Sure?"

"Yes, yes, take it," she confirmed, extending the set of keys to him.

When they approached the wrought-iron door to the left of the altar, Derek silently inserted the key into the lock and turned it. The door opened almost soundlessly and closed a moment later, allowing the "tomb explorers" inside. They didn't turn on the general light to avoid attracting attention;

someone from the castle could be looking out the window at this time. Megan turned on her phone's flashlight, which provided sufficient lighting.

The young man confidently led the way forward, as if he had been here hundreds of times. Even if he walked in the dark with his eyes closed, he would not have made a single mistake in navigating towards the required burial. After about fifty steps, he stopped. A small nook of about fifteen square meters branched off to the right of the corridor. On its left side was Margaret's tomb, and opposite that, rested her mother — two large sarcophagi on heavy stone legs. As the couple approached the correct one, all of Megan's courage evaporated in an instant, and she said, "You were right, this was a bad idea. I think I overestimated my strength. Let's go back, take me to my room, and then you can come back and explore everything without me. You're not afraid… I mean. We should have done like this from the start. Why didn't this idea come to me earlier?" She clutched Derek's forearm with an iron grip, pulling him back.

"That's it? Is your courage over just like that?" he asked, raising his right eyebrow with a smile.

"Yes, I'm terrified, please, let's just get out of here quickly," she pleaded with him.

"Come on, don't be afraid, I'm here. Everything's okay."

"There's nothing near the burial site, and it's unlikely we'll find anything. It was foolish to think we'd find some clue here."

At that moment, it seemed to the girl that dozens of eyes were watching her back. She was terrified to turn around and see a living-dead extending their arm towards her.

She knew this wasn't a horror movie, but she couldn't help herself. After finding out that a person can turn into a raven, anything seemed possible in this world. Megan's heart was pounding wildly. She was about to follow her companion, but, taking a step into the corridor, Derek suddenly pulled her back. Footsteps were heard — someone was entering the crypt at that moment. The young man snatched the phone from the girl's hand and turned off the flashlight, managing to press his finger to his lips, signaling her to be silent. Both leaned back against the wall. Megan felt a surge of fear inside. Thoughts flickered through her mind, one after another. Who is it? Gregor? Did he see someone enter the chapel and decide to check? A ghost? Maybe a dead person rose from the grave? A killer?

The footsteps were getting closer.

Derek, sensing that his beloved was about to scream from terror and timely covered her mouth with his hand. Someone was walking very slowly, trying to find where they were hiding. This someone was intentionally searching for them. Derek's entire body was tense; he pulled a small dagger from behind his waistband — a gift from his father, which he always carried with him. Megan saw the blade flash in the darkness, and at that moment, the footsteps stopped. Whoever was behind the wall had figured out their location. Derek immediately lunged at the pursuer with the dagger, not giving him a moment to react. The assailant, who was clearly expecting a defenseless woman, jumped at the sight of this opponent. The girl's legs seemed glued to the floor; she now covered her own mouth to hold back a scream. Overcome with horror, she heard them fight a life-or-death battle. First, there was a shout from a male — not Derek — followed by a gunshot. Then the pursuer screamed again and hurried towards the exit of the crypt.

Megan heard loud, dragging steps receding into the distance, peeked into the corridor, and saw a limping figure rushing to leave the place. He wore the same black cloak with a hood, as he did on the night of the first attack. Searching for Derek with her eyes, the girl saw him sitting on the floor, leaning against the wall. He was holding his left forearm with his right hand. She rushed to him and realized that her savior was wounded. His right hand covering the wound was bloodied. Megan's teeth chattered, her emotions growing stronger and stronger. She screamed, her voice tinged with hysteria, "Derek! You've been shot! Is the wound only on your arm? Or somewhere else?"

"Just on the forearm...he had a gun. There it is," he nodded towards the weapon lying nearby. "I struck him with the dagger twice, he's also hurt."

"You need a doctor immediately!" tears streamed from the girl's eyes.

"What are you talking about? I don't have any identity documents, and this is a gunshot wound, do you understand? The police will get involved. I don't exist on paper, remember?" the young man gritted through his teeth.

"So, what do we do?"

"Help me take off my jacket and bandage the wound. We need to stop the bleeding."

"Do you know how to do it?" Megan asked, hoping for a positive response since she had no idea how to properly bandage wounds.

"Yes, I guess," Derek sighed heavily.

Following his instructions, the girl said, "Please forgive me, it was my foolish idea that led to this tragedy. You were right not wanting to come here."

"There's no point in tormenting yourself with guilt, nothing can be undone. And if not today, he would have ambushed you another time, and who knows how that could have ended. He came here for you and didn't expect to encounter a man who could fight back. You're in danger, Megan, don't go out alone anymore, even during the day," he warned her.

"I don't understand who could be behind all this and why, but we can discuss this later. The main thing now is your wound. How do we get the bullet out? God, what should I do? How can I help you?" she sobbed.

"Don't worry; I'll take care of myself. The main thing is to get home as soon as possible."

"But how will you get there? You can't fly like a raven; you'll have a wounded wing."

"I'll go through the secret passage, after I escort you."

"How are you going to escort me with an open wound?! Are you out of your mind? I'm the one who will see you off," Megan protested, her hands trembling as she helped him bandage the wound.

The look he gave her said a lot.

"Derek, don't you realize you're losing a lot of blood? You could die!" she continued, panicking at the thought of the worst possible outcome.

"I won't let you go alone. Do you understand that you're in danger?" he retorted angrily.

But she continued to argue, "He won't be back today. He's hurt too; he won't bother chasing after me now."

"Megan, this is not up for discussion," he concluded firmly.

"Do you have any medical supplies at home?" she asked, realizing she couldn't persuade him.

"A bit…"

"Tomorrow morning I'll go to the pharmacy in Thurso and buy everything you need. The wound must be cleaned and treated properly. Stay with me, so I can help you."

"That's very risky; someone could find me there."

"I won't let anyone into my room," Megan pleaded.

"But you don't have the necessary medicine now; you can only buy them tomorrow. But I have something, plus the bullet needs to be removed, so we need tools," Derek said.

"Do you have alcohol to treat the wound?" she asked, helping him put on his jacket.

"Yes, don't worry," Derek handed her the remnants of his shirt which was torn for bandaging, "Wipe the blood off the floor with this; we need to clean up the traces of this incident, or Warren and Gregor will have many questions about what happened here. We don't need that right now. Here, in the crypt, it won't be clear what these stains are. The floor is uneven, and the lighting is poor. And in the church, you need to wipe everything down thoroughly. Then wet the shirt with water that's at the altar, and wipe it down again," he instructed her.

"I'll do it quickly. Just don't move, you can't afford to expend energy."

In five minutes, she managed to completely clean the blood traces in the church as much as she could.

"Let's go," said Derek, getting up.

"Derek, don't even think about seeing me off!"

"Megan ..." his look was adamant.

"All right then, you stand at the church door, and I'll run to the castle. As soon as you see that I've entered, you can go home. If something happens, you'll be able to come to my aid. But you can't afford to waste your strength walking back and forth, understand?! Otherwise, you won't make it home. You'll run out of strength halfway there."

"Okay, go," he agreed, feeling weaker with every passing minute.

"My love, how will I know everything is alright with you? You don't even have a phone."

"I have no one to call, so I don't need one. Don't worry about me; all will be fine. I'll come to you at seven tomorrow. Go love, everything is okay," he lifted her chin with his finger and quickly kissed her lips.

They had to say goodbye quickly; he already felt dizzy from the blood loss.

"How can I find you if something happens to you?" said the girl, wiping away the tears that rolled down her face.

"Megan, go. Nothing will happen to me. It's just a small wound."

"Derek, don't try to calm me down; you think I can't see how serious this is?"

"Everything's fine, I've already told you. Please go, we can't stand here forever; your relatives might see us."

He turned her towards the castle with his healthy hand, kissed her on the top of her head, and nudged her forward.

She took a few steps then heard him call after her, "Please, don't go out alone during the day, it's very dangerous right now. Promise me."

"All right," Megan replied and ran towards the castle.

Once in her room, she went straight to the bathroom. What she saw in the mirror was horrifying. Her face and hands were covered in blood; she had smeared herself when wiping away tears with bloodied hands. Megan quickly started stripping off her clothes, eager to step into the shower and wash away all traces of this terrifying ordeal. She couldn't sleep at all until midnight, wondering who wanted to kill her. How could this nightmare happen? What worried her most was Derek's injury. She was very anxious about whether he could make it back to the castle. Horrible images haunted her; of him lying on a hill, half-way from home, completely alone and weakened. With incredible effort, she forced herself to banish such terrifying thoughts.

18
Anxiety

Waking up in the morning, Megan decided her first order of business was to head to the pharmacy. Despite all of her beloved's warnings, she couldn't just sit at home worrying about whether or not he had all the necessary medication for treatment. One could go mad and start hating oneself for such inaction. And in the evening, when he would come, she would be able to give him all the anti-inflammatory and antibacterial agents for further therapy. She had made a list of necessities overnight, fearing she might forget something.

Calling a taxi and quickly getting ready without having breakfast, she went to Thurso. Upon leaving the house, she encountered no one, thus avoiding any awkward questions about where she was going and why. Arriving at the pharmacy, she asked the driver to wait for her. Fortunately for Megan, the pharmacy was staffed by a very pleasant woman who recommended adding a few extra supplies to those on her list. An issue arose when purchasing an antibiotic, as the pharmacist was reluctant to sell it without a prescription. However, Megan pleaded with her, convincing her it was for her sick dog suffering from a severe wound. The woman eventually relented. She herself was a dog lover and sold Megan the antibiotic, albeit surprised that a veterinarian hadn't issued a prescription. At that moment, for Lord Drummond's girlfriend, it didn't matter what others thought of her, nor how she obtained the antibiotic, the important thing was that she got it.

Back at the castle, Megan met Glenn coming down the stairs.

"Hi, Megan! How's everything?" she asked languidly.

"Hi Glenn, everything's fine. How about you?"

"I overslept a bit today. I'm not feeling very well. I guess I'm starting to come down with something."

The young woman indeed looked unwell.

"It's not surprising, such unpleasant weather. Chilly, and continuous rain, cold winds…you really shouldn't go out right now. You need to rest up. Drink hot tea with lemon and ginger. And vitamin C would be essential right now."

"I'll tell Warren to buy some," Glenn said.

"If you need anything, just let me know. Maybe bring lunch to your room?"

Glenn shook her head.

"Go lie down then, I'll check on you periodically."

"Thanks, Megan, you're a true friend. I'll have some tea and then go to bed."

"Then let's have tea together, I haven't had breakfast yet. After that, I'll walk you to your room. You look really pale; I don't like it."

*****

Megan was restless, worried about Derek. She couldn't wait for the evening to come to ensure he was okay. Additionally, throughout the day, she visited Glenn several times, whose condition was seriously concerning. Megan had never seen her friend so weak and lifeless. Glenn had refused the lunch brought to her, citing a complete lack of appetite. Megan barely managed to persuade her to have a few spoonfuls of chicken broth.

Warren returned from the distillery late but stopped by the pharmacy on his way back, as his cousin had insistently requested over the phone, and bought vitamins for his wife. When he saw Glenn's condition, he became worried and decided that if she didn't get better the next day, he would have to call a doctor.

Megan and Warren had dinner together at six in the evening and then retired to their rooms. Anxiety gripped Megan even more when Derek didn't show up by seven. By eight o'clock, she was in complete panic. Something serious must have happened; Derek was not someone to break a promise. If he said he would come at seven and didn't, it was alarming. Every five minutes, she went to the window, hoping to see him outside, but in vain. Megan sat on the bed and covered her face with trembling hands. She imagined the worst scenarios. She feared that while trying to extract the bullet, he lost too much blood and couldn't stop the bleeding, so was now unconscious or worse, dead. Or perhaps the assailant who attacked them had ambushed him on his way back and killed him.

"My God, what should I do?" Megan moaned aloud, her imagination still racing with all sorts of horrible scenarios.

Sitting like this for a quarter of an hour, she realized that this was no time for hysterics and that she needed to act. She had to find Derek immediately, learn what had happened to him, and try to help. But the question was: how to find him, how to get into his room? She tried to recall the conversation when he explained where he lived. About the secret passage that led to his bedroom. She quickly got dressed, grabbed her phone, and dialed the necessary number. The dial tone seemed to go on forever.

"Megan, hi! What's up? Is everything all right?" Duncan finally asked, slightly surprised.

"Hi! Yes, everything's fine. How are you?" she tried to make her voice sound as carefree as possible.

"All's good."

There was a moment of silence. Duncan was waiting for her to speak. Megan had clearly not called just to ask how things were; she had a purpose.

"I thought I'd take you up on your offer to come over for a sleepover, if you and Alaric don't mind."

Megan blurted out, praying to herself that he wouldn't refuse.

"Of course, come over, no objections. Are you sure everything's okay? You previously categorically didn't want to accept my invitation. And now this, so suddenly," Duncan's voice became concerned.

"I just got bored, wanted a change of scenery and to take the opportunity to find a book in your library that I've wanted to read for a long time. I remembered your invitation and decided to accept it now. I called immediately to not give myself time to change my mind. Anyway, I'll be there in fifteen minutes. Thank you, Duncan," she blurted out quickly, so her cousin wouldn't change his mind either.

"Okay, I'm waiting for you. I'll go tell granddad that we will have a guest."

"Thanks again."

Duncan's voice clearly conveyed his surprise at such a turn of events. Her action was beyond the norms of decency. To call in the evening and ask to visit, more precisely, to boldly declare that she would be there in fifteen minutes — it was too much. At this moment, she couldn't care less about etiquette or what her relatives might think. Derek's life was in grave danger, and she needed to find him urgently, no matter the cost.

Packing all the necessary medicine, a bottle of whiskey as a substitute for alcohol, and just in case, a clean sheet for bandaging into her bag, Megan went in search of Gregor to ask him to drive her to Castle Raven. He was extremely surprised by this request, but of course, did not object. He only asked anxiously if everything was alright there. Or had something happened to Alaric? Pretending to be completely calm, she assured him that everything was fine, and that she was simply fulfilling a promise she'd made long ago to her relatives to come by for a sleepover.

*****

"Megan, my girl, what an expected surprise!" said the master of the house, his face showing a surprised look, as soon as she crossed the threshold.

Alaric was dressed in a bathrobe, apparently ready for bed. It was about ten in the evening, and people in Castle Raven tended to go to bed early.

"My apologies for such a late visit. I understand it's somewhat untimely, as usual, such things are arranged in advance, but it just happened spontaneously."

She felt completely foolish, realizing how silly this must be sounding. At ten in the evening, a young relative suddenly deciding to spend the night with them? Regardless of how she felt and how it all looked, Megan was firmly and persistently pursuing her goal.

"It's okay, you can feel at home here, I've already told you that. Now let's go have some honey tea. It's good for the night. Then Duncan will show you to your room," said Alaric.

"Thank you."

Megan offered the old man a warm smile, though internally she was a bundle of nerves. Wasting precious time on tea and meaningless conversation was the last thing she wanted to do. But she understood the importance of honoring their hospitality. Paying them ample attention would help ease the awkwardness of the situation. They might think her mad if she announced she was heading straight to the library or to bed instead of having tea. She had to wait until they dispersed to their rooms before searching for Derek. Most importantly, she couldn't be caught prowling the castle in search of the secret staircase, as that would lead to serious trouble. It would be utterly embarrassing. Thus, she had to engage in calm conversation, lulling their vigilance, and then the entire night would be hers to search.

As Megan took her seat at the table, Duncan appeared in the kitchen.

"Good to see you again!"

She picked up a distinct note of sarcasm in the statement. Apparently, her unannounced late visit was not entirely to his liking.

"Glad to see you, too, Duncan; it's been a while," she said, trying to make light of the situation.

Duncan and Alaric sat down opposite her. A tense silence hung in the air; both sets of eyes were fixed on her.

Megan frantically thought about what to say, needing to quickly diffuse the tension and end the awkward silence.

Finally, she spoke up, "The weather has turned so bad these last few days, I've stopped going out of the castle. It became very lonely and dreary. I remembered how nice it was yesterday in a warm family setting, and felt the urge to come to you. Warren and Glenn are spending the entire evening in their room since Glenn has fallen ill. The boredom and loneliness were just driving me crazy.

Duncan looked at the girl with some suspicion. He didn't quite believe what she was saying but couldn't fathom the true motives behind this odd visit. Alaric, however, easily believed Megan, and in a fatherly manner, began to talk about the importance of having a family, and that their doors are always open to her at any time.

For another hour, they talked about family, Megan's return to London, and she emphasized again how accustomed she was to a very active lifestyle. Now, with the weather turning bad, she had lost the opportunity to do anything and was struck by a bout of melancholy.

Duncan relaxed a bit after these words; it seemed he believed his cousin, who appeared to be somewhat whimsical and crazy from boredom and idleness.

Having finished their tea and looking at the clock, Alaric said, "I'm used to going to bed early, so please excuse me and let an old man rest."

"Good night. Thank you for the company and hospitality."

Duncan followed his grandfather's example, "Come on, Megan, I'll show you your bedroom and then head to bed myself, if you don't mind? I have an important work matter to attend to tomorrow morning."

19
In Search of Derek

Left alone, Megan first pulled the sheets off the bed — in case the hosts discovered her absence from the room, she'd let them think she spent some time in bed. After waiting another half-hour, she very quietly opened the door and tiptoed downstairs, without a sound. From Derek's description, she remembered that the secret passage is near the side staircase of the tower. The difficulty lay in how to find it. She very much hoped it would not take too much time.

Approaching the tower staircase, she did not turn on the lights to avoid attracting anyone's attention. She did not know if the cook or any other servants were asleep in the castle and feared being seen by someone. Turning on her phone's flashlight and looking around carefully, she saw neither a door nor a passage. Panic started to set in: what if she got it wrong and it wasn't the right staircase or tower? If she couldn't find the passage...couldn't find her beloved, then what? He would die, and she would never see him again. Walking around the staircase again, illuminating every section of the wall, she found nothing. She felt very sorry for herself.

Why me? Why do all these trials fall onto me?! Life was calm and peaceful, and then suddenly — everything turned upside down in an instant. Pull yourself together, think Megan, think! There must be an entrance somewhere. Don't panic, Derek is not in a good situation right now, she mentally urged herself.

As always, having reasoned with herself, she examined the space around her once more. Apart from the staircase, and an old cabinet built into the wall, there was nothing else. Then she carefully opened its doors, every moment with fear that they would creak and wake everyone up, but thankfully, no creak followed. Examining the contents closely, Megan saw only a few mops and a plastic bucket. A thought flickered that the door might somehow be camouflaged in this closet. She started to explore the walls with her hands, focusing especially on the back. Intuition told her the passage was right here. She pressed hard with both hands and… the wall gave way. The girl barely kept her balance, almost falling down the staircase that suddenly opened up to her. Closing the hidden door behind her, she lit the steps with her flashlight, relieved that her search was successful. The stairway passage was quite narrow. One part led down, the other up. Lighting the walls and ceiling with the beam, hoping not to have a spider or rat fall on her, Megan slowly started to ascend. Adrenaline surged, her heart pounding wildly in her chest. She clutched her phone like a lifeline, afraid to drop it and be left in utter darkness. An eerie silence surrounded her.

After climbing a couple of floors, she'd assumed, something small and solid fell on her head. "Jesus!" the girl squealed, frantically shaking it off her head. She nearly went into full-blown hysteria. After a few minutes, having made sure that nothing was crawling on her by feeling every part of her body, she started to climb again, faster. Tears of fear and desperation were streaming down her cheeks. Finally, Megan reached the top floor, where there was a door. She prayed that there wouldn't be any locks and pulled the doorknob hard, but it didn't budge. Then she pushed the door with her shoulder, and it swung open....

Megan found herself in a storage room full of old, unwanted furniture. Along the walls, there were several rows of cabinets, secretaries and dressers. There was hardly any space left, which made it difficult to move around. She was shocked and disappointed by what she saw. The abundance of cobwebs and centuries-old dust suggested that Derek couldn't possibly be here. What if she had mistaken the tower and it wasn't the right staircase? "Oh God, what shall I do?" the girl prayed. She started to look around, perhaps there was another entrance somewhere? Maybe her beloved's room was located next to this one? Megan walked counterclockwise, examining every cabinet inside and out. Thoughts whirled through her head. She remembered the conversation about his dwelling; Derek had mentioned that his bedroom was located in the left tower. So, this is the left tower from the entrance. He couldn't have considered the castle from any other angle. So, everything was correct, she was headed in the right direction. On the way up, there definitely weren't any other doors; she had carefully examined the walls. This meant the entrance to his room must be somewhere here. She pushed the inner wall of each piece of antique furniture, hoping that one of them would turn out to be a secret passage — that seemed logical to her. But so far, nothing has been working. After checking half the room's furniture, she stopped, feeling something move on her shoe. In panic, she began to shake her foot and shine the light on the floor. And saw a mouse, equally frightened, scurrying away from her.

"Bloody hell! Now, I'm definitely going to lose my mind," she sobbed. Her nerves were on edge. Not knowing what to do to keep her sanity, without screaming and crying on the floor, she opened her bag, took out the bottle of whiskey, and took two big gulps. Closing the bottle with the cork, she put it back in her bag. On trembling, faltering legs, she grabbed onto the nearest piece of furniture to avoid falling, and continued her search. In one of the cabinets along the wall to the left of the door, where there were many old dresses with ruffles, the girl felt a round hole in the back panel. Initially, she tried to push the panel, but it wouldn't budge. Then Megan inserted her index finger into the hole and pulled the panel towards herself. The secret door swung open, revealing yet another door in the wall. The girl realized that this was it — the entrance to Derek's room. All that was left was to hope he hadn't locked himself in, considering the state he was in. Fortunately, her fears were unfounded. She took a few hurried steps forward...

The lamp in the room was dim, but its light was enough to see a single bed on which Lord Drummond lay... motionless.

A wave of horror washed over the girl from head to toe. Jesus! Is he dead? She rushed to her beloved and touched his face with her hands. It was burning with fever. Thank God, he's alive, tears once again streamed down Megan's face. Conflicting emotions raged inside her: fear for his life, stress from the past hour... and joy that she had finally found him.

"Derek, can you hear me? It's me, Megan," she gently tapped his uninjured shoulder.

The young man did not react. He lay shirtless, his torso bare and vulnerable. Next to the bed was a basin with water, which was red with blood. Apparently, he had been rinsing the wound and had rebandaged it with a white cloth, but something had gone wrong. The girl feared for blood poisoning. She carefully untied the bandage on his forearm to see the condition of his wound and saw that he had stitched it up. Shocked at how he managed to do this alone, she hoped that the needle and thread were well sanitized before the procedure. How he sterilized them was beyond her comprehension. Or perhaps he hadn't sterilized them at all, which could lead to a catastrophe — the risk of sepsis was incredibly high.

Growing more and more distressed, Megan took out the medicine she had brought with her. In her entire life, she had never administered first aid to anyone. She had never encountered any kind of trauma, except for a minor knife injury in the kitchen. The sight of blood usually puts her in a semi-fainting state. But apparently, life has decided to test her fully and confront her wildest fears. Taking a clean white cloth, she soaked it in whiskey and carefully wiped the inflamed area, shaking a few extra drops for an enhanced effect. Derek felt the pain, moved slightly, and moaned softly. But he did not wake up. He began to shake with fever; muttering something incomprehensible, as if delirious. Megan covered him with a blanket that was by his feet. Taking out the antibiotics and a fever reducer, she crushed them into powder, mixed them with a spoonful of water, and poured the mixture into her beloved's mouth, slightly lifting his head. He coughed a bit but did not come round. His temperature was incredibly high. She estimated it to be no less than forty degrees Celsius. She had to wait for the fever reducer to take effect and the antibiotic to stop the inflammatory process that had started in his body.

Taking a basin, she went to change the water. The bathroom was clean and tidy, except for the carelessly scattered bloodied cloths. It was evident that Derek himself was a fairly neat person who liked order. However, he felt so ill after the incident that he tossed the bandage materials haphazardly on the floor. This broke Megan's heart. The bathroom, like the entire room's setting, dated back to Lord Drummond's youth. Megan thought it was natural: he couldn't have ordered new furniture to be brought into the castle under the watchful eyes of her relatives.

Filling the basin with cool water, the girl returned to the bed to apply a cold compresses to his face — combined with the fever reducer, they could help lower the temperature. Sitting next to him, she placed a wet cloth on his forehead which heated up within seconds. She kept dipping the cloths back into the water, repeatedly changing the compresses. Glancing at the clock, she counted the minutes, waiting for the temperature to start dropping. But there was no sign of improvement. One more time Megan checked all the medicine she had brought; it was too early to give paracetamol again, she had to wait at least two more hours.

Taking the antibacterial powder, she inspected the wound, which had already dried, then sprinkled it with the powder and carefully wrapped it with a sterile bandage. Gently embracing Derek, she mentally tried to transfer some of her strength and health onto him. Someone had told her that one person could draw energy from another, and she wholeheartedly wished for it to work now. About twenty minutes later, the fever began to decrease. The medication started to work. But throughout that night, Megan's protector remained unconscious.

Dawn approached, it was 5:30am, and the girl didn't know what to do next. Without proper care, he wouldn't recover. Leaving him here alone meant leaving him to die. But she couldn't stay with him either. What would her relatives say if they didn't find her in Castle Raven or Castle Mal?! Or if she requested to stay another day or two as their guest… and then vanished again into the secret chambers and got caught? That is definitely not an option — her relatives would think she had completely lost her mind and that they should stay away from her. But what then? How can I stay with him without arousing any suspicion? Nothing logical came to mind.

Derek felt a bit better after the second dose of fever reducer that she gave him about two hours ago. Dawn was near, and when he becomes a raven, giving him another dose of medicine will be impossible. She hoped that in the form of a bird, it would be easier for him to endure this ailment.

Megan had been so consumed with the condition of her beloved Highlander, that she hadn't really taken a good look around his room. She surveyed it with great interest. The bed on which the young man lay was situated about a meter from a tiny window, opposite the door.

To the left of the bathroom, stood a large bulky wardrobe, opposite it was a desk on which she saw a laptop. Megan didn't expect Derek to have a computer, especially since he didn't even use a phone. But there was nothing strange about it: he had no one to call, and a computer is needed for various tasks. Moreover, Lord Drummond was quite advanced in all knowledge, having modern views on various topics. When he recovers, she would definitely ask him what he needs a laptop for. As she thought this, she glanced at the tiny window in the tower, through which only a raven could indeed fly.

Dawn was getting nearer. Megan continued to ponder what to do with her unconscious beloved, how to proceed. She couldn't leave him alone, but she also couldn't raise the suspicions of the relatives due to her inexplicable behavior. It was about time to return to her bedroom; otherwise, she risked encountering someone in the hallway.

Suddenly, Derek's whole body trembled violently, his face contorted in pain, he groaned and a black whirlwind hovered over the bed. Megan recoiled in fright, pressing her hands to her chest. It was the moment of transformation from human to raven. The girl had witnessed this transformation before, but since the reality still hasn't fully sunk in, it caused her no less horror. A few seconds later, the black veil over the bed dissipated, and a raven now lay on the bed. Megan crept closer and called his name. The bird did not stir; it lay lifeless, not opening its eyes.

In that moment, a clear understanding of what needed to be done came to her. The decision came naturally. Opening the wardrobe and finding a clean sheet inside, she wrapped the lifeless body of the raven in it, trying not to hurt the injured wing. Hanging the bag on her shoulder and turning off the dim lamp, she switched on her flashlight and took the same path she had followed a few hours earlier.

Now she was no longer afraid. She thought about not accidentally hurting the fragile body and hurried to Castle Mal so that the injured would not freeze to death. Before leaving the wardrobe, Megan slightly opened its outer door, checking to see if the coast was clear. Assured that all was quiet, she came out and immediately headed to her assigned room to tidy up the bed before leaving to see Derek. Then she went downstairs, and at that moment, saw Duncan entering the dining room. She followed him to pay her respects and greet him before saying goodbye. It was impossible to leave without saying a word after they had shown her such warm hospitality.

"Good morning, Duncan! You're up early," Megan said, with a strained smile.

"Good morning, Megan! I have an important meeting today. And what's that in your hands?" he asked curiously, stirring his coffee.

"A strange noise awakened me this morning. It seemed like someone was knocking on the window. Taking a closer look, I discovered an injured bird that was seeking help. When I opened the window, a raven with a broken wing fell right into my hands. I felt so sorry for it; I'm on my way now to Castle Mal — I want to treat its wing and then let it go."

Duncan looked at the bird with disgust and took another sip of his coffee, "Cousin, you are so kind and caring. Good luck! I hope you manage to revive it. Would you like some tea?"

"No, thank you, I'll be going now. I just wanted to thank you and Alaric for the hospitality. Please, pass my heartfelt thanks to your grandfather as soon as you see him."

"Of course, but there's no need to thank us, as my grandpa said, this is your home too. Should I drive you to Castle Mal? It's cold outside, you'll freeze."

"That would be great, Duncan, thanks," the girl was relieved.

"Let's go, then."

He glanced once more at the bundle in Megan's hands, shook his head in disbelief and smiled at her.

She didn't care what he thought. Her main task was to get back to her room as soon as possible. Only there would she feel safe.

When she appeared in Castle Mal, she met Gregor downstairs. He tried, with interest, to see what she was carrying. After greeting him, she quickly passed by without giving him a chance to understand what was in her hands. Warren and Glenn were probably still asleep. Megan decided to see her cousin-in-law a bit later, sincerely hoping she was feeling better. Once in her bedroom, she carefully placed the raven in the middle of the bed. Looking at it, she searched for signs of life. The only thing giving her hope was that it was warm. Other than that, it remained motionless.

Megan was very glad about the fact that daylight had become shorter and in eight to nine hours, the raven would turn back into a human. All she could do was wait.

At ten in the morning, after locking her room, she went to Glenn. She was feeling significantly better but had not yet fully recovered.

"Has Warren already gone to the distillery?"

"No, he went to meet with Duncan. They have an important business affair today."

"Have you had breakfast?"

"Not yet, no appetite," Glenn grimaced.

"Well, you have to eat anyway; otherwise, you won't have the strength to recover."

"I know. I'm ready to drink some tea and eat a small muffin. That's all I can manage."

"All right, give me a second; I'll bring it to you," Megan headed towards the door.

"No, no, don't bother. I'd like to go down to the kitchen myself, no point in lying in bed all day," objected Glenn, getting up from the bed.

"Okay, then let's go together, I haven't eaten yet either."

Over breakfast, Megan mentioned her visit to Castle Raven. The cousin-in-law was quite surprised.

"If you did that, you must have really been bored here. I hope the change of scenery helped you to unwind?" Glenn smirked.

"Yes, a lot. The only problem is that I couldn't sleep in a new environment, so I think I'll go to bed early today... at around six," the girl said, preparing an excuse for her absence at the upcoming dinner.

"Right, you need to catch up on missed sleep."

"Exactly," Megan smiled.

She didn't want to share the story about the raven with anyone, hoping that Duncan would soon forget about it too. That way, no one would ask any questions about the raven.

20
Back to Life

Megan spent the entire day in her room, leaving only for lunch to the kitchen. She had a quick meal alone, as Glenn was taking a nap at the time.

The girl counted the hours and minutes, eagerly awaiting sunset. When it finally came, Derek was lying on the bed. His temperature was still high but not as dangerously so as the day before, she noted with relief. Her first action was to change his dressing with antibacterial treatment and give him his medication. Lying next to him, waiting for the effect to kick in, she fell asleep. Her exhaustion from the previous sleepless night took over.

Her sleep was so deep that she didn't immediately hear Derek calling her. Megan lifted her head and looked at the clock on the mantelpiece, it was two o'clock.

She touched Derek's forehead to check for fever and was overjoyed to find that his temperature had significantly dropped.

"Thank God! You've regained consciousness!"

"Megan, what am I doing here? How did I get to you? The last thing I remember, I was treating my wound in my room. Then I must have blacked out."

"You didn't come the day before yesterday, as you promised. I was terrified and went out looking for you. I found you a little over a day ago. You were unconscious, feverish, with a high temperature. I brought all the necessary medication with me and started to treat you. I was so afraid for your life; at one point, I thought I would lose you."

"And how did I end up here?" he asked, frowning in displeasure.

Megan took a deep breath, knowing her beloved would not like what he was about to hear.

"The fever didn't drop all night. I couldn't leave you alone; you wouldn't have survived. And I couldn't stay there with you, I would have been suspected. It was already a huge effort to spontaneously ask Duncan and Alaric if I could visit. Imagine, if I showed up late in the evening out of the blue, wanting to stay the night. And when you turned into a raven, it became clear what needed to be done."

Derek's face showed clear dissatisfaction. The feeling of his own helplessness left a bitter taste inside. Reading these emotions on his face, Megan said, "You were on the brink of death, do you understand? In my place, you would have done exactly the same. So, there's no need to act like Mr. Groucho right now. You're alive, and that's what matters most right now. You need proper care to recover quickly. And until that happens, I'm not letting you go anywhere. And if I need to handcuff you to the bed or put you in a cage, believe me, I will do it for your sake. You need to be alive and well. Got it?" she insisted, leaving no room for argument.

He looked at her in amazement.

"So, I'm your prisoner, then?"

"Call it whatever you like. If you like the word "prisoner," then you're my prisoner until you recover. I'm not prepared to go through that fear again."

He sighed deeply and asked, "Did it take you a long time to find me?"

"No. Thank God you told me where the secret passage was."

"I left all the doors open just in case," Derek recalled.

"You did well, otherwise I doubt I would have managed."

Raising an eyebrow and smirking at her, he said, "You would have."

Then his gaze became serious, "Megan, your life is in danger. This is the second attempt on you. He will return once he's healed. If not him, then someone else."

"I understand, but it doesn't add up in my mind who could be behind this," she said hopelessly.

"I think it's quite clear; it's about your relatives. If you're gone, the inheritance goes to them. Who else benefits from your death? Or do you have serious enemies in London, too?"

"But I warned them that I would inform my lawyer, and if anything were to happen to me, there would be a serious criminal investigation. You'd have to be a fool not to understand the problems this could cause. And I can't even imagine who among them could do this! Or do you think there's a conspiracy? Like, Warren, Alaric and Duncan... could all three be conspiring to kill me?" she said, unwilling to believe her own words.

"After the first attack, I've been watching Alaric and Duncan closely, but that topic never came up. They talked about you with a lot of sympathy among themselves. I think Warren has the most to gain here. He manages all your property but only gets half. If you were gone, he'd get all of it. So, I think he's the most suspected party in this matter," Derek expressed.

"Logically, yes. But Warren seems to be the kindest, most open, and sincere of them all. He's the type of person who wouldn't hurt a fly. I can't believe he's capable of this."

"Megan, please be very careful around him. Don't be alone with him."

"I can't accept that yet. Couldn't you see the attacker's face?"

"No. He was probably a hitman. It's highly unlikely any of your relatives would personally dirty their hands with blood — literally. As soon as I recover, I'll spend all my daylight hours watching Warren. And once we solve our problem in November, I want us to leave for London immediately. There, we'll figure out what to do next."

"You're right. But the most important thing now is that you get well as soon as possible."

"I'm hungry," Derek changed the subject after a brief pause.

"Of course, you haven't eaten in two days. Wait, I'll give you food I brought from the kitchen today."

Megan quickly got up from the bed, took a bag of food from the mantelpiece, and began to take out sandwiches, fruits, cookies, handing everything to Derek in turn.

"Thank you, my love, but wait, I won't eat all this. Give me one sandwich and an apple. That will be enough for now. You've taken care of everything. What would I do without you?!"

An hour later, Derek felt a loss of strength again and quickly fell asleep. Soon after, his temperature rose. Before going to sleep, he took the medicine she gave him, except for the fever reducer. Megan was glad that he had finally come round. Now, with proper care and adherence to bed rest, he would recover quickly. Before going to sleep herself, she poured the medicine into Derek's mouth to help reduce the fever.

*****

The following few days, caring for Derek, passed very quickly. He felt better and better each day. On the third day of his stay in Megan's room, the fever completely subsided, and his temperature no longer rose above normal. Lord Drummond wanted to return to his own room, but Megan insisted on waiting at least another day. She also convinced him to refrain from any physical exertion. Not wanting to cause her unnecessary worry, — Derek conceded.

On the fourth night of his stay at Castle Mal, he said, "In the morning, when you wake up, I'll be gone. Don't worry about me. I'm in perfect condition thanks to your attentive care. We'll meet in the evening, but I'll be late, around ten or eleven o'clock. So, don't go looking for me, okay?"

"Alright, but what will you be doing until so late?"

"I have some matters to attend to."

"What matters?"

"Total control?" he asked, laughing.

"I saw the laptop in your room. What do you need it for?"

"For work."

"Work?" she asked surprised.

"I need to manage my income somehow. You can't get by without a computer these days," Derek explained, not understanding her surprise.

"But where do you get income from?" Megan asked, even more astonished.

"Stock markets."

"How is that possible if you don't exist on paper? There are accounts and you need documents for those," she puzzled, furrowing her brow.

"I've got them," Derek calmly replied.

"You what? So, we could have gone to the hospital after you were wounded? Do you realize how much you risked by not doing that? What if you had gotten a blood infection?"

"My documents are very old; according to them, I am 89 years old. The hospital would hardly believe they were mine. And no one on the stock exchange knows me; no one sees my face. It's time to get new documents. Such issues are usually resolved in big cities. London is perfect for that."

"Yes, we'll take care of it as soon as we get there. I'm glad you have some sort of occupation; I must admit, it really shocked me," she said, looking at him admiringly.

"Just because I don't have a phone doesn't mean I'm not keeping up with the times, or stuck in the 19th century. It's just that I have no one to call. But as soon as we move to England, I promise I'll get one. Anyway, technology is advancing and soon it'll be necessary, not just for making calls but for work too; it will completely replace computers."

"Super," Megan approved of this decision.

"Although, I've got no idea when we would actually call each other. When I'm human, I'm always with you, and a raven can't speak," Derek teased her with a smile.

She looked at him sternly, "Let it be so. It makes me feel more secure knowing that you have one."

"As you wish, my queen," he said, kissing her.

*****

"Megan!" Glenn called happily, as she ran into the kitchen.

"Glenn, dear, what happened? Clearly, there's no fire in the house," Megan turned around with a smile.

"Warren and I have just received the results of my test! I'm pregnant!"

"Oh, my God! Glenn, I'm so happy for you! What wonderful news!" Megan exclaimed, embracing her friend.

Warren appeared in the doorway following his wife, smiling from ear to ear. Megan hugged him as well and expressed her sincere congratulations. They had been waiting so long for this and were overjoyed by the news. Watching them was a sheer delight.

"How far along are you?" Megan inquired.

"Four weeks. Warren is going to call his brother and grandfather now. We'll invite them over for dinner tonight and share the news. They'll be thrilled, especially Alaric, who wanted to live to see a great-grandchild and was so upset that neither Warren nor Duncan had children."

"That's wonderful! It's going to be a great evening!"

On the one hand, Megan was sincerely happy for them, but on the other, the thought that one of those gathered around the dinner table that evening could be a murderer wishing her dead, cast a shadow over her mood.

"My mom will also come," Glenn's voice pulled Megan back to reality.

"Have you already told her?"

"No, you're the only one who knows so far. I couldn't be near you all day without sharing such news, I'm just bursting with happiness. I called my mom in the morning, told her that we're having a very important family dinner and she absolutely must attend. Naturally, she got worried and asked what was going on. I reassured her that everything was fine."

"What's your mom's name?"

"Ginny. I miss her so much. She's so kind and sweet! I'm sure you two will get along. Will you come for the baby's birth?"

"Sure! I wouldn't miss it for the world!"

"I'd like you to be the godmother," Glenn said with a pleading look.

"Oh, that's so unexpected," her friend said, taken aback, not sure how to react.

"Do you mind?"

"No. Of course not. I'll be the godmother if you really want me to," Megan replied with a smile, still not sure whether she liked the idea or not.

She had never been a godparent before, and she didn't really have much experience with children.

"Warren, did you hear? She agreed! Craig will be the godfather! How wonderful! Though Craig doesn't know yet."

"So, you're due in the summer? Which month?" Megan started counting on her fingers.

"You don't have to count. The baby is due in the last week of June," Glenn answered.

"It's been exactly one year since I first arrived here," observed Megan.

Warren listened to the women while sitting at the table picking grapes from a bunch on the dish, smiling broadly.

*****

As the sun started to set, a taxi pulled over by the castle. A young, attractive woman in a beige coat stepped out. A joyful Glenn ran out to meet her.

"Mom!"

"Sweetie, what's happened? Tell me what is going on! You've never called me so urgently to a family dinner," her mother asked excitedly.

"Let's go, I'll take you to your room, we'll sit down there and talk about everything."

In the hall, a pleased Glenn introduced her mother to her best friend, "Mom, meet Megan, Warren's cousin. She's now the lady of Castle Mal. And this is my mom, Ginny, the best mom in the world," Glenn affectionately hugged her mother.

"Hello, Ginny, it's a pleasure to meet you."

"Hello Megan, likewise. My daughter has told me a lot about you. I'm very glad she's found a friend here," Ginny responded with a friendly smile.

In front of the girl, stood two women; the resemblance was uncanny. Both were of medium height, with well-proportioned figures. Glenn's blond hair, as always, was tied up in a bun. Ginny's hair, of the same shade, was styled beautifully. Both had pleasant, open faces that were inviting, and kind eyes where the joy from seeing each other was easily read.

"I'll leave you for a short while, you have things to discuss," Megan winked at her friend. "See you at dinner."

The evening was wonderful. No one in the family could have imagined that such a moment would come, and they would all be together celebrating this event. The anticipation of the baby for the couple had been prolonged to such extent, that hope had faded, and few believed that the sounds of a child's laughter would once again fill this home. Alaric was so moved that he couldn't hold back his tears, and Glenn's mother was overwhelmed with happiness. She was immensely joyful at seeing her daughter's shining eyes and shared her elation.

Throughout the evening, Megan enjoyed the atmosphere of familial bliss, momentarily distracting herself from thoughts of the conspiracy, to prevent them from overshadowing today's news. She couldn't fathom that people capable of such profound positive emotions could harbor such dire intentions. The atmosphere of mutual understanding and warmth enveloped everyone, especially Glenn, who received special attention and love from all.

"That's great news, Megan! Warren told me you agreed to be the godmother!" said Duncan.

"Yes, I'll come for the baby's birth, and then we'll have the christening."

"Why isn't the godfather at the table?" Duncan asked his brother.

"Craig is out of town. He'll be back in a few days, and I'll tell him the news then."

"Do you remember what today's date is?" Alaric changed the subject, and without waiting for an answer, continued, "All Saints' Day is coming soon. I hope no one will refuse to have a great time?"

"How is it celebrated here?" Megan inquired.

"Oh, it's one of the most ancient, mysterious, and ominous festivals in our history. It was celebrated by the ancient Celts. Of course, it's not as grand as the fern flower festival, but it's certainly interesting. The main difference is the masquerade costumes of all kinds of supernatural beings! Witches, vampires, werewolves, goblins, zombies... you name it! We, the old folks, wear traditional kilts, while the youth — whatever their imagination comes up with. The main purpose of this event is to dispel evil spirits with unrestrained merriment, to rid ourselves of them. So, it's time to think about outfits! We'll have a contest for the most terrifying one!"

"I think this celebration will be even brighter here than in Edinburgh!" Megan joyfully supported Alaric.

"Edinburgh can't compare with us! Prepare your costumes and come over early. We'll show you a real All Saints' Day!"

Dinner lasted until late, and Megan only managed to get to her bedroom by half-past eleven. When she emerged from the shower, Derek was already in the room. She had missed him a lot throughout the day, having gotten used to his constant presence. His absence today was particularly felt.

Derek approached her, gently embraced her, and kissed her neck.

"How was your day, love?"

"Good, and yours? No fever? And how's your arm? Any pain?" she asked with concern.

"No. I feel great," he was amused by her excessive care.

"I'll change your bandage, and you need to take an antibiotic."

"Do the bandage, but I think I don't need the antibiotic anymore."

"Don't even think about it. You've got to complete the full course of treatment."

Derek sighed deeply, "Arguing with you is futile. Give me the antibiotic so we can forget about it. You'll make me take it one way or another."

"Here you go, and some water to wash it down. You know, we had a big celebration today — a family dinner."

"What's the occasion?"

"Glenn has been unable to get pregnant for many years. Today, the tests confirmed she's expecting a child. You can't imagine how happy she and Warren are."

"I can imagine. Warren will have an heir, so he's even more interested in getting rid of you to take everything for himself."

Megan, frowning and said, "Derek, I know how all this looks, but I don't believe it's him. Warren is a very good person. And especially since he and Glenn had given up hope of having a child. He definitely hasn't planned a murder based on the idea that something would go to his heir."

"Time will tell who it is. I think I'll find some information in a couple of weeks." Derek didn't argue further, although his opinion remained unchanged.

"Glenn asked me to be the godmother," the girl said with a smile, brushing her hair in front of the mirror. "She's due in June, and I need to come here for the birth to stay for the baptism."

Meanwhile, the young man, adopting a casual pose, lay on the bed tossing nuts into his mouth from a bowl on the bedside table. Looking at Megan, he asked curiously, "Would you like to have your own children soon?"

Megan was taken aback by the question. Seeing her confusion, he raised an eyebrow in surprise and asked, "No?"

"In the future, yes, maybe, but definitely not anytime soon. Children are a huge responsibility, and we don't even know what will happen to us after November 12th. We don't have stability in our future right now."

In truth, the prospect of motherhood didn't please her at all, and she tried to choose her words carefully so as not to disappoint.

"Agreed."

"And what about you?" she asked, holding the brush and looking at him through the reflection.

"What about me?"

"Do you want kids?"

"In the future, yes, after I've taken on a normal form and we've sorted out all the formalities. But I can't say it'll be in the near future. For now, I'm not ready to share you with anyone else," he said, smiling at her reflection in the mirror.

This greatly reassured Megan, who feared having discussions about the need to have children.

"What did you do today?" Megan abruptly changed the subject, feeling uncomfortable discussing anything related to motherhood.

"I can't say I got a lot done, as I didn't have much time, but I managed some things. By the way, I did a bit of surveillance on Alaric today, but didn't hear anything interesting. Spent a little time on Duncan, but that was in vain, too. I'll dedicate the next few days to Warren."

"I really hope we find some answers soon," Megan said with a heavy sigh.

"Of course, we will, just give me some more time."

"Derek, we need to plan everything carefully for November 12th. The day is approaching. I'm thinking of going there once in advance, it will help me to physically and mentally prepare for the big day. What do you think?"

"Let's go there in the morning. I advise you to dress very warmly! The weather is miserable at the moment, always raining and windy."

"Yes, I know. Tomorrow I'll look for a hotel near the Ring. I'll tell my relatives I need to go to Edinburgh for work for two days."

Derek sat on the bed, "The plan is this: around ten in the morning, you'll leave the house and head to the island. Take a taxi to the port; no one should see you off. I'll join you on the ferry. We'll get there by daylight, take a look around, and then return ten minutes before midnight."

"I wonder in what form the answer to the question will come. Will a voice tell us what to do, or will the answer come in some other form?" Megan pondered thoughtfully.

"I don't know, let's not think about it for now. Just remember, I'll always be by your side, don't be afraid," with these words, her beloved stood up from the bed, hugged her waist from behind, and kissed her shoulder.

"What do you think about Halloween? Alaric mentioned at dinner that they'll be celebrating it, following all the traditions. We need original themed attire, and I have no idea where I can find a costume in time."

"Hmm, I'm not sure now is the best time for such festivities, but if you really want to…I know what costume would suit you perfectly. So, if you'll allow me, I'll choose and bring it to you," Derek offered, not particularly thrilled about the prospect of Megan going costume-shopping with ome family member.

"I'm curious to see what you've picked out for me!" she smiled.

"Don't you think we've been spending too much time talking lately?" he asked, kissing her neck.

"You were sick; what else could I do with you?" she said, turning to him with a mischievous smile.

"I'm not sick anymore," he said between passionate kisses.

"I missed you so much."

"I missed you too…" he said, leading her to the bed.

That night, like the following nights full of passion and love, brought Megan and Derek closer to the most important moment of their lives. The girl was no longer afraid; she eagerly awaited the November night of revelations. This night separated her present from the future. She couldn't wait to get the answer and leave with Derek for London, where they would start a new life as a normal couple. These dreams gave her the strength to endure the dull, monotonous days at Castle Mal. Summer here was incredibly beautiful and comfortable. But in late autumn and winter, during the strongest winds and rains, it was cold, damp, and dreary outside.

21

Halloween

Days slowly succeeded each other. The incessant rains and icy winds finally made Megan a prisoner of the vast castle. The entire week leading up to Halloween, she constantly tried to keep herself busy, to somehow distract herself from thoughts of their uncertain future. Thus, she started planning a new design for her restaurant in London. The capital's restaurant needed to keep up with the times, so she spent hours on her laptop, carefully exploring various interior options. She repeatedly discussed her ideas with Sam, who thought her decision was premature.

Periodically, she still visited the library. Here, Megan dedicated time to studying Scottish culture, specifically its Celtic origins. Deep down, without fully realizing it, she hoped to find an answer to the question about Derek's situation.

Due to the dreary gray weather and the memories of the recent attack still fresh in her mind, the girl failed to notice everyone living and working in the castle. Now, she only crossed paths with Glenn and Warren at breakfast and dinner. The happy face of her friend was the only thing that illuminated the gloomy days in the castle.

Every subsequent day was like the previous one, until the day before the holiday when Glenn peeked into Megan's room, "I got so caught up in my own concerns that I completely stopped visiting you. I'm sorry, I feel so ashamed about it..." the future mother began to apologize.

"Don't worry about it. You should be taking care of yourself and the baby right now."

"I've been visiting doctors all week," Glenn began with a bit of annoyance, "so I haven't managed to fully think through my look for Halloween. Are you ready for tomorrow?"

Megan wasn't particularly thrilled about the upcoming event, so she hadn't really thought about it, until Gregor brought her a costume box. As promised, Derek had arranged for its delivery. But she hasn't yet had a chance to see what's inside.

"Yes, I'm all set! Do you need any help from me?" she asked her friend.

"Yes, I can't figure out what to do with my hair. I wanted to let down my bun, but it seemed too simple," Glenn looked hopefully at her friend.

"Let it down, we'll think of something," Megan gestured towards the vanity table. She had never seen Glenn with her hair down before, so she commented, "Your hair is incredible! Why do you always hide it in a bun? I can make you a French braid. Or we could just take two side strands, weave them together at the back, and leave the rest loose," the girl said, sifting through her friend's hair.

"Hmm, I think the second option is exactly what I need! Thank you so much! What would I do without you?"

"Oh, it's nothing, you know I'm always happy to help. By the way, what are our plans for tomorrow? How is the event going to unfold?"

"Tomorrow after lunch, we'll prepare everything necessary for the celebration, and then we'll slowly start getting ready to go. This year the party will take place near Castle Raven."

A few minutes later, they said their goodbyes, and Glenn fluttered off to her affairs. Megan watched the door close behind her friend in a thoughtful silence until a rustle at the window drew her attention. Spinning around, she saw her beloved.

"Derek!" Megan instinctively threw her arms around him.

"Glad to see you too," he smiled, hugging her back.

Then releasing the embrace, the young man looked at her with a serious expression, "Megan, I'm worried about you. We don't know for sure if that guy won't take the opportunity to attack you again. Tomorrow everyone will be in carnival costumes, with faces hidden under masks. I understand it's a party, and your relatives will be there, but please, be careful. Don't stray from people; if someone asks you to step aside with them, find an excuse to avoid it."

Megan looked at him sadly.

"You're right, I was thinking about that too. I promise not to go off with anyone, don't worry," she said stroking his cheek.

*****

Waking up early in the morning, Megan felt lively and full of energy. She easily got out of bed, took a shower, dressed, and went downstairs for breakfast.

"Good morning!" Glenn, in her joy and vitality, seemed to surpass herself.

With quick movements, she served Megan a plate of eggs, bacon, and beans, along with a cup of coffee, and fixed her beaming gaze on her friend. Bursting with impatience, she continued, "It won't rain today! So, the Halloween party should be perfect!"

"That's great news! Where's Warren?"

"He's off on some business; then he'll pick up my mom and bring her here; they'll arrive just in time for the event. Meanwhile, you and I will have time to prepare the sweets and lanterns!"

"Wow, we've got a busy day ahead of us," Megan said, sipping tea from her cup and trying to seem interested in the celebration.

At that moment, Glenn's phone rang and she left the kitchen, finally giving Megan the chance to have breakfast in peace.

During the day, the girls carved jack-o'-lanterns out of pumpkins and turnips prepared in advance by Warren. For Megan, this was a new experience; she had never carved creepy faces before. But while engaged in this activity, she discovered that this was a rather entertaining and creative pursuit.

Duncan stopped by around half-past one to collect the lanterns to decorate the venue where the festivities would take place. He reminded them that he and Alaric were eagerly awaiting their arrival in the evening and hurried back to the castle, where he had to add the final touches to the festive atmosphere.

Meanwhile, the girls distributed a mountain of candies into bags for the youngest Halloween guests. After dealing with all these pre-festival preparations, Megan and Glenn parted ways for a while.

Megan took the box previously brought by Gregor and placed it on her bed. Carefully unwrapping the paper bags in which her carnival costume was packed, she was amazed at how meticulously Derek had selected each detail of her outfit. He even included lipstick and eye shadow! She marveled at his attention to detail and hurried to try on her unusual attire.

She put on everything that was in the package, including the makeup, and walked over to the large mirror in the room; she couldn't wait to look at the image Derek had envisioned for her.

Megan was dressed as a forest fairy. She was wearing brown high-heeled Cossack boots, a floor-length emerald-green gown embellished with various flowers and autumnal leaves, and a dark green hooded velvet cloak. A garland of white flowers and green leaves adorned her head. Megan was awestruck by what she saw in the mirror. Now she looked just like a Scottish forest fairy, fresh off the pages of the folktale books she had been reading not long ago.

Hearing a commotion in the hall, she went downstairs, where she saw Glenn and her mother Ginny.

"Who's that?" exclaimed Ginny in surprise. "It would seem that the forest fairies themselves live in this castle," she remarked, admiring Megan's costume. She was dressed in a classic kilt.

"The forest sprites have found shelter in the stone halls here, too!" Megan sauntered down the stairs to greet her guest. "Happy to see you again!" She carefully hugged her friend's mother, trying to keep her unusual headdress out of harm's way.

"Mutual, dear! Your costume is stunning!" praised Ginny.

"I have to agree!" Glenn supported. "Now it's clear what you've been pondering this past week," she joked.

Warren dressed as an ancient warrior. Black pants tucked into high boots adorned with iron spikes and trimmed with fur. A knee-length black shirt embroidered with whimsical golden patterns was cinched with a wide leather belt. On it, in a scabbard, hung a large sword. The outfit was complemented by a long warm cloak in blue-green plaid and a fur collar. His wife wore a floor-length black dress with the same golden pattern as on her husband's shirt. A small dagger hung in a scabbard on her belt, accentuating her waist. Her russet hair was let down and, on her head, sparkled a graceful golden tiara. On her shoulders, just like her husband, was a long woolen cloak in blue-green plaid. Warren and Glenn perfectly complemented each other.

"Guys, you look magnificent!" Megan announced, admiring them.

Fifteen minutes later, Alaric greeted the festive procession at Castle Raven. This year as well, he didn't dare abandon the traditional Scottish costume.

Megan was about to greet him, but at that moment something touched her shoulder. Before she could turn her head, Alaric said, "Wow, our forest fairy has learned to befriend wild birds! Now that's what I call an image!"

Megan quickly realized what had happened, but this time, didn't resist it. A black raven was sitting on her shoulder.

"It's all the power of ancient magic!" concluded the owner of Castle Raven.

On the meadow, many fires of various sizes were burning — for conducting different rituals. In ancient times, their purpose was to protect this land from evil spirits.

Megan overheard someone near a fire, speaking in a soothing voice, explaining to the youngest guests, "The Celts believed that on this night, their deceased ancestors would return to the world of the living, but along with them, evil spirits could also come. To scare them off and keep them at bay, many fires are lit. To make the spirits mistake them for their own, or to scare them away, men and women would dress in frightening costumes."

The girl didn't linger in one place; curiosity pulled her further. She watched with interest as people in whimsical costumes sang songs, performed wild dances, and scared each other. Bagpipes played everywhere — their shrill sound, according to old beliefs, also drove away evil spirits. This was Megan's first time attending such a celebration. It was nothing like the Halloween parties organized in cities. Reaching the center of the clearing, she saw two tall, bright bonfires. Between them, women and men walked alone, or in pairs, whispering quietly.

"It's an ancient purification ritual," explained the man next to her. "They seem to be reciting a prayer or a spell…"

Megan looked in surprise at the man standing to her right. He was dressed as a vampire.

"Duncan! I didn't recognize you at all," she laughed.

"Sorry love, I thought you'd have no difficulty figuring out it was me," he smiled with his vampire grin.

"Truly a worthy inhabitant of an ancient castle," Megan remarked ironically.

"I hope that's a compliment?" Duncan tried to conjure up something akin to a friendly smile. "I've been wondering, is that raven on your shoulder real or stuffed," he asked, reaching out towards the bird. But he quickly recoiled as the defender of the forest fairy struck the offender with its beak, quite aggressively.

"What are you doing?" Megan said, anxiously addressing the bird perched on her shoulder. "Duncan, I'm sorry. It didn't hurt you; I hope?"

"No, no, it's all right. Your raven guards you well!" Duncan smiled back, though he looked at the bird with disfavor.

That's for sure, she thought.

"Come on; I'll take you to where the fun's really at! You should see how they divine on Halloween!"

Megan gladly followed her cousin to where the young men and women gathered for divination. They threw chestnuts into the fire and watched their placement. If two chestnuts burned together, it meant the diviners were to spend their lives in love and harmony; if they rolled apart, then it wasn't meant to be.

At one of such bonfire, Megan spotted her favorite warrior-clad couple. She was curious about what fate had in store for them. She approached just as Warren and Glenn each threw a nut into the fire. Megan closely watched as the nuts fell into the flames and, rolling towards each other, slowly burned in the tongues of fire. Shifting her gaze to the warrior, she saw a concentrated, serious expression on Glenn's face, which became softer and kinder with every passing minute.

"Their life together will be long, peaceful, and happy," commented Duncan. "If the nuts burn with a crackle and hiss, or if they explode, then you should expect constant quarrels and scandals."

Megan felt that everything should be fine for Glenn and Warren. Watching her friend's reaction, she couldn't help but wonder: How would the nuts have burned if Derek and I had thrown them? The raven, as if reading the thoughts of his enchantress, pressed his body against her neck. The fairy gently scratched his wing in response.

Glenn and Warren joined the forest fairy and the vampire.

Approaching the tables set up for Halloween, where eerie characters were already drinking and snacking, Megan noticed the pumpkin lanterns they had carved with Glenn in the morning. With candles placed inside, they looked ominous. Among the reveling adults, children dressed in scary costumes of ghosts, mummies, and other supernatural beings, running around, shouting, "Trick or treat?"

The friends observed the contestants for a while longer then moved towards the large bonfire, where everything was ready to conclude the night. After spending a couple more hours at the party, Megan was dreaming of returning to her room. After saying goodbye to Duncan and thanking Alaric for the amazing evening, Warren, Glenn, and Megan went to Castle Mal.

All they had the strength for once they reached the castle, was to wish each other a good night. After dispersing to their bedrooms and taking off their costumes, they fell into their beds and fell asleep.

22

The Ring of Brodgar

The long-awaited November day had arrived, when their fate was to be decided. Megan put on the warmest clothes she could find in her wardrobe, not forgetting her favorite white hat with a pom-pom and winter mittens. She had previously informed her relatives about a short business trip. When Megan said goodbye to Glenn at breakfast, Warren had already left, which she was immensely relieved about. She feared he would insist on taking her to the station, where she wasn't intending to go.

Ordering a taxi, Megan headed to the port, and only then did the first apprehensions about the risky venture they had decided on, start to accumulate. Her main fear was not about how everything would go or how scared she would be, but the possibility that they would not find answers and would not be able to return Derek to a normal life. What then? How would they carry on? She rode to the port, praying silently for higher powers to help them, to give them an answer on how to lift the curse, and for it to be within their power. The night before, Megan noticed Derek's anxiety for the first time, though he did not express his fears in words. His pensiveness and silence revealed his inner turmoil. He was out of sorts; his face was overshadowed by a gloomy, dark expression all evening. This was quite natural, considering that his life, their common freedom, and future were at stake. His fears matched his beloved's anxieties: what if they don't find answers, what if the midnight ritual doesn't work? The closer they got to the decisive moment, the more fear enveloped them. They pinned too many hopes on this night, which might not come to fruition.

Arriving at the port, Megan purchased a ticket and headed to the ferry that was to take her to the designated place. She looked around in search of the raven, but it was nowhere to be seen. It became cold on deck due to the strong wind, and soon she decided to go inside to warm up. Twenty minutes later, Megan went out again in search of the raven, but it still did not appear. Anxiety overcame her, Derek always kept his word. If he promised to accompany her, he should be hear; if not, something definitely must have happened. Another ten minutes passed, and she again took shelter inside the ship.

The girl was plagued by anxious thoughts about what would happen if he did not show up. As soon as the ferry docked, she went outside, and at that moment, a black raven made two circles above her head. She breathed a sigh of relief, Thank God, he is here, and aloud added, "Derek, by the way, I was worried! Where have you been? I was freezing while going out on deck looking for you."

A couple passing by gave peculiar looks to Megan, who was still frowning at the raven. But the girl did not pay attention to them. Upon arrival, she first went to the hotel, situated as close as possible to the Ring of Brodgar, which she had booked in advance. She took the keys to her room, changed her clothes, and went back outside. The raven was sitting on the fence near the hotel.

"Let's go, we need to see how long it will take to get to the ring," she said to the raven.

Megan walked silently, immersed in her heavy thoughts. Periodically, she looked around to check if anyone was following her. But there was no one around. It felt like she was alone on the entire island. Despite the cool weather, the beauty of the surrounding landscapes impressed her, and Megan was glad that it was not raining. Approaching the stone circle, she found herself feeling as if she was observing everything from the outside or dreaming a strange dream. All these mysterious events, the magic she had previously feared and did not believe in, now seemed utterly real to her. Standing in the center of the stone circle, she saw the raven make a wide circle above it, surveying the area. Megan extended her right hand forward and called the raven with a gesture. The raven landed on her hand and looked into her eyes with a long, meaningful gaze. Gently stroking it, she said, "We'll make it, you'll see! Everything will be fine! We've been waiting for this moment for so long. You've earned your freedom, and you'll get it! May the one who did this to you turn in his grave."

The raven turned its head toward the altar. It was a very thin stone slab in the center of the ring. Megan approached the slab to examine it more closely. Everything was more or less clear to her, and she saw no need to linger much longer. She turned and headed towards the hotel, intending to have lunch there and wait for Derek's transformation.

When her food was served, she tried to stretch out the meal to somehow pass the time, instead of sitting idly alone in her room. Having eaten well and feeling satisfied, she ordered a large cup of tea, followed by a mug of coffee. When Megan finished her coffee, it was getting dark outside, so she went back to her room.

For about twenty minutes, she sat there motionless, staring at a single point with an almost unblinking gaze. And then he appeared. He sat next to her on the edge of the bed, turned his face towards her, kissed her, and, taking her chin between his two fingers, looked into her eyes, "Are you scared?"

Megan, with a note of anxiety in her voice, replied, "I'm only afraid of doing something wrong and not getting a result. Or doing everything right but still not getting a result. What if I can't connect with this cosmic force or whatever it is?! Then what? I'm not afraid of anything else."

"Everything will work out, you said so yourself today. I believe everything will be alright," Derek said, though deep down he was engulfed by profound fear.

His own fears tormented him; he couldn't predict what awaited Megan after this night. This night could radically change her life. She might face the unexpected, and it was unclear if she would be able to forgive him for the trials ahead. Fear, heartache — he didn't want to think about the future. At this moment, he wanted to lose himself in her embrace, forgetting everything in the world. He hugged her tightly and kissed her again. Megan, pulling away from his lips, began to gently kiss his eyelids, forehead, cheeks, and then said, "Derek, I love you. You are my life. And no matter what happens, I will always be by your side."

He sighed heavily and, hugging her tightly, rested his head on her shoulder, pensively looking out the rain-drenched window.

*****

"What time is it?" Megan exclaimed in a panic as she opened her eyes. She couldn't believe how she could fall asleep on such a crucial evening. After long, passionate caresses from her beloved, she was lying in his arms and unexpectedly fell into a deep sleep.

"It's half past eleven. I was just about to wake you," Derek reassured her.

"God! I was so scared that I slept through the most important night of my life. Did you sleep?"

"No," he calmly replied.

"We need to hurry. It's more than a half-hour walk in the dark. We can't be late! Better to wait there an extra fifteen minutes."

"Arriving too early isn't good either. You'll freeze, and who knows how long we'll have to stay there after midnight."

Some time later, they left the hotel and headed towards the Ring of Brodgar. It was very dark, and occasionally there was a strong wind. They walked in silence, each lost in their own thoughts. Approaching the altar, Megan took a sealed sterile medical syringe out of her bag.

"Some heroin for courage?" asked Derek, trying to lighten the mood.

Megan laughed, somewhat breaking the heavy atmosphere.

"What time is it?" she asked.

"Five minutes to."

She removed her mittens and pulled out a bandage and an alcohol wipe. Then she cleaned the skin on her left wrist and made a small puncture with the needle. After performing the ritual of sprinkling the altar with blood, she lay on top of it. Derek sat to the right of her shoulder, at the head of the altar. Megan took a deep breath and looked up at the sky, waiting for the unknown. It felt like an eternity, although she lay for no more than three minutes. Surrounding her was silence…nothing happened. She listened carefully to her inner sensations. But there was not even a hint of change. Then she closed her eyes, and after a couple of seconds, everything in her head began to swirl, as if she was being pulled into some kind of vortex. Fear distorted her face, and she clenched her fists tightly, but did not open her eyes.

Time and epochs changed, the girl lying on the stone slab felt both heat and cold. Millions of thoughts flashed through her head — familiar and entirely new, as if belonging to someone else…voices. Visions flew before her eyes like frames of a movie: laughter, tears, joy, pain, happiness, love. She was immersed in Derek's past, living his life alongside him. In that moment, Megan was filled with a deep, pure love for

Derek, and joy from their shared existence. She was struck by his bright, cheerful laugh — so happy and carefree, unlike anything she had heard from him during the months of their acquaintance. His eyes shone like never before. Megan dived deeper and deeper into her feelings and sensations. She found herself in that time when he was young and happy, and it wasn't a memory for her but a reality in which she now resided.

Meanwhile, Derek couldn't take his eyes off her face, sitting at the head of the altar. His facial muscles tensed. He wished he could know what was happening to his beloved right now and how long it would last. Her face periodically relaxed, showing complete serenity, then tensed again, and she clenched her teeth and fists.

Minutes dragged slowly. A tumultuous range of emotions once again reflected on the girl's face: first fierce anger and disdain, then deep sorrow. Tears streamed from her eyes. She was seized by hysteria, convulsively writhing on the altar with closed eyes and moaning.

"Megan!" her beloved quietly called, fearing she might hurt herself.

He tried to hold her by the shoulders to prevent her from falling. Her hat slid off her head. Without opening her eyes, Megan rolled onto her right side and fell to the ground next to the stone slab. She lay motionless. Derek gently lifted her, holding her close like a child, her head resting on his shoulder. He hugged her, quietly calling her name. Her face showed no emotion; she did not respond to his voice. In that moment, Megan was in a deep oblivion. After a few minutes, she came round, opened her eyes, and directed an empty, almost glazed look into space.

Derek quietly called her again. She turned her head to look into his eyes.

"Forgive me! Forgive me, my love, for cursing you, condemning you to a life full of agony."

Pain was frozen in her eyes.

From heart to heart:

Dear friends! I wholeheartedly thank you for sharing the exciting journey of Megan and Derek through the pages of the epic fantasy saga "The Magic Ring of Brodgar."

This thrilling story, unfolding in two parts, has not left readers indifferent. I sincerely hope that the images of the main characters - courageous Megan and noble Derek - resonated in your hearts. If this book touched you, please share your impressions in the reviews on the website where you purchased this edition. If you made the purchase in a bookstore, I would be delighted to see your opinion about it on literary forums and platforms. I eagerly look forward to reading the words from each of you, dear readers. I am grateful in advance for the time spent and the sincere emotional response expressed in your reviews. You are the ones for whom I wrote this saga.

Katelyn Emilia Novak
www.themagicringofbrodgar.com
Instagram: Katelyn.emilia.novak

Printed in Great Britain
by Amazon